Drumming Up The Dead

My Paranormal Experiences

Jéan Boomer Grenier

Boomerjnk Publishing

My Paranormal
Experiences

DRUMMING
UP THE
DEAD

Jean Boomer Grenier

FOREWARD BY LISA DOWALIBY
Member Of New England Anomalies Research
& Former Cast Member Of SyFy Series Ghost Hunters

This first edition published September 26th, 2024
by Boomerjnk Publishing

Editors : Kara Roger & Nina Walden

Cover Design By : Jéan Boomer Grenier

Forward By : Lisa Dowaliby

Paperback Book ISBN : 979-8-9916687-0-5

Hardcover Book ISBN : 978-8-9916687-1-2

eBook (Kindle) ISBN: 979-8-9916687-3-6

eBook (EPub) ISBN: 979-8-9916687-2-9

Copyright © 2024 Jéan Boomer Grenier & Boomerjnk Publishing

Library of Congress Control Number: 2024922023

US City Of Publication ; Nashua

Printed In The United States Of America

Printed Paperback & Hardcover Books By : Amazon KDP

Global Distribution By : IngramSpark

For more info please visit ; jeanboomergrenier.com or jboomergrenier.com

DRUMMING UP THE DEAD

This book is dedicated to my loving wife Kerry, my parents Maurice and Carol, and to my close family and friends that have passed on. Especially to the ones that have been back.

John & Helen Janerico
My Grenier Family Aunts & Uncles
Louise Grenier
Steven King
Jarrod Wallace
Chris Messier
Mike Hagen
Greg Thomas
David C. White
Michele "Mickey" Kanan
Pete Fortes

Contents

Foreword

By Lisa Dowaliby

It's often said that music unites people. That's very true, but what if you add the paranormal into the mix? Perhaps even a dash of veterinary medicine? Sounds like a pretty strange combination.

Be that as it may, it's sort of a summary about how I became friends with Jéan "Boomer" Grenier and his wife, Kerry.

We met on a cold February day in 2011. We were at a paranormal fundraiser for a very young girl who was afflicted with a life threatening illness. I was a guest speaker, and the Greniers were donating some of Jéan's KISS memorabilia for auction. My husband, Ray, is a fellow musician as well as a huge KISS fan, so we immediately struck up a conversation once I saw the items Jéan had brought. The other crazy coincidence was that Kerry and I are both veterinary technicians! Instant friendships were made that day, and have endured since.

As we spoke, Jéan began relaying some of his personal experiences with the paranormal. He was so matter of fact, yet detailed in his descriptions. He explained the way he could sense things when others seemed oblivious. It occurred to me that musicians in particular have a unique sensitivity to the abstract and sensory world around us. Throughout history, many cultures have used music as a doorway to the beyond, and an aid to contact or invoke spiritual beings. The energy and feelings that are carried with music are, indeed, very similar to what people describe when they have contact with the spirit world. Happiness, love, anger, sadness, are all heard and felt as tangible energy, particularly to those who have creative minds.

One of the most frequently used musical instruments for spiritual ceremonies is the drum. That's really no surprise, when you think about it. Drums are, essentially, the "soul' of the music - they carry the vibration, the pulse, the mood of the song. Their power to be both foreboding and uplifting gives them a unique sort of impact. Jéan is a professional drummer, having decades of experience in the music industry. I truly believe that his musical talent and sensitivity to the spirit world are intertwined.

Jéan's compilation of stories are just like the man himself - down to earth, matter of fact, yet unique and thought-provoking. When reading his accounts, you get the feeling that you are hanging out with a friend, listening to his stories in his own voice. That's one of my very favorite things about this book - it's like that first conversation I had with Jéan. Interesting, down to earth, fun, and relatable.

I hope you like this book as much as I did. Paranormal books are by no means rare, but this one has a vibe all its own.

Get comfortable in your favorite chair, turn on your music, and enjoy *Drumming Up The Dead*.

Lisa Dowaliby & Myself

Lisa is a former case manager for The Atlantic Paranormal Society (TAPS) and former cast member of the SyFy series Ghost Hunters. She also holds a degree in anthropology and is currently a member of New England Anomalies Research.

Introduction
What The Hell Is Going On?

I believe at an early age I had and still currently have a "gift," if you will. Unfortunately, it's not something I can easily control or call upon at will. I've always been creative, which is why I'm a lifelong musician. Taking art lessons when I was around nine years old, I was decent at sketching and drawing with pen and ink, but even earlier than that, music was what really moved me. I would sit in my room by myself and draw, listen to music, and let my mind wander. Life seemed so much easier back then, riding my BMX and playing sports with friends. But when I looked at the lives of my friends and schoolmates, I quietly noticed glaring differences. My friends would say they had dreams about participating in specific activities or doing certain jobs when they grew up. I'm not talking about aspirations, but the acts of actually going to sleep, dreaming, waking up, and remembering their nightly dreams. I didn't have that. I didn't think it was a big deal or anything out of the ordinary at the time, I just figured I was earning some solid sleep.

One part of my young life that I do remember is the boy. For about a year or so, I had a very close friend. I would sit in my room and a little boy, who was maybe five or six years old, would be there with me. We'd talk to each other and play with Hot Wheels cars. Periodically, my mom would ask me whom I was talking to, but I only knew him as "Little Boy." He was passed off as a normal, childhood imaginary friend. He never bothered me or was malicious, he just provided company for me, which, as an only child, I appreciated. Eventually, he stopped showing up, and I completely forgot about him until years later. I believe he's still around and not imaginary at all. He seems to be a much bigger part of my story.

As I grew into my adolescence, I noticed situations a little more but wrote them off as explainable or I just ignored them altogether because I really didn't believe in ghosts or the afterlife. To me, ghosts were just spooky symbols of Halloween or objects to scare people on TV and in movies. They certainly weren't real. Later, I discovered I was dead-wrong about that as well. As for my dreams (or lack thereof) when I sleep, this continues ... with one exception: I have premonitions. I can go months and months without ever remembering any dreams, but once I wake up and remember one, I now pay very close attention to whatever details I can recall. Usually, if I have the same dream over consecutive nights, an event tied to that dream seems to happen not long afterward. If it's a "one-time dream," I ignore it.

The first time I was able to confirm that what I was possibly experiencing were premonitions instead of dreams was related to a violent crash in 1987. I had the same dream a couple of nights in a row. It's not something I thought about after waking up. The ensuing day was completely normal, but when I drifted back to sleep that evening, I had the dream again. Within days afterward, there it was on the news: two huge Amtrak trains collided in Maryland. After that, I woke up, so to speak. I began paying more attention and asking myself a bunch of unanswerable questions. Was there another realm? Were there people there? Was someone there attempting to condition me for what would continue throughout my life? Was it a way to potentially gain information, a way to help the living before something terrible happens, or a way to confirm that I have some kind of communication from the other side? I didn't know, and honestly, I still don't. In the meantime, I've received messages and passed them along. I've been shown images and I've been told information I could have never known on my own. Again, it's a "gift" I can't control. It just happens.

I decided to write this book for a couple of reasons: to share my true experiences with the paranormal and some unexplainable situations that have stuck with me for one reason or another, and to hopefully help or enlighten others. I feel maybe not everything in our current lives as we live is meant to be explained now. I was never a believer in ghosts, but I can tell you today as I write this, there is something more going on than just our "living" existence. I am now a firm believer in the paranormal and the fact that we are not alone. I wasn't alone in my room listening to music when I was a child, and I know I'm not alone in my room now as I type this sentence. My mother passed four years ago, and her lighthouse urn sits on a shelf six feet away from me. She is here and I sense it.

My hope with these true stories I've encountered is that if you already believe, maybe it will solidify that you, at one or more times, have also encountered something you can't explain. A loved one that has passed, a cry for help from beyond, or just a strange situation that leaves you bewildered. Nothing that says you are crazy but in fact proves that you are not. If you are not a believer, then maybe after reading this book you may consider when you're alone, opening your eyes and mind to the notion that maybe you're not alone. There's a possibility that just because people have passed doesn't mean that they are not in your life anymore. That means family, friends, a person you've never met, or a person who lived previously where you do now. Remember, for all those living today there are more that have passed and the living are outnumbered.

CHAPTER 1

There's Uncle Arthur!

My father had fifteen siblings: ten sisters and five brothers. I know the question you might be pondering - yeah, there was one bathroom. The family had to eat dinner in shifts. If one of them missed their time slot, they were out of luck and had to fend for themselves. Of the family, there were two brothers and a sister who lived together. My Uncle Arthur, Uncle Alberic, and my Aunt Simonne were known as "The Travelers," as we'd always receive postcards from them from all over the world. One month it would be from Egypt, and then the next from Portugal. Every once in a while, it would be from some place stateside. Another aunt, Antoinette, was a Catholic nun. She was a bookkeeper for an orphanage in Vermont until she moved to do the same job at an orphanage in Quebec, Canada, where she later resided full time. Aunt Antoinette, or rather "Sister," as we would call her, would come home on holidays or vacations to visit family and stay with The Travelers on the third floor of the three-tene-ment apartment building on Salem Street in Lowell, Massachusetts. The three-story building that was her home base was also home to two other aunts and their families. I will never forget the creepiness of the long, creaky staircase that wound up to the third floor. There was always very low lighting, or none at all, when climbing the stairs to any of the apartments. Sadly, the building has since been torn down to make room for the expanding hospital next door.

My Uncle Arthur was a stoic man, and most of his nieces and nephews (myself included) always thought he was in a perpetual bad mood. He had constant resting bitch face for a man. He may or may not have been in a sour mood, but oftentimes he definitely looked quite cranky. I honestly don't remember many conversations with him because I stayed clear of him whenever he was around. In all honesty, Uncle Arthur never said or did anything mean to me, or to anyone I knew. I'm sure my other cousins would have spilled the beans if something had happened to them, but I never heard anything. My Uncle Arthur religiously wore black slacks, a white tank top undershirt, and he walked with a cane. He was always dressed exactly the same whenever I saw him. I used to think he had seven identical outfits, one for each day of the week.

Uncle Arthur was talented. In his workshop that adjoined his bedroom, he would make string art designs. He made a Superman string art for me. For my mom, he made a tall ship with large sails. They were pretty awesome, just nails and tacks affixed to a wood backing with different color strings intertwined to create the picture. He used to give them as gifts. The only time I remember Uncle Arthur smiling was when he'd present one of his art pieces to us or someone else in the family. He was very proud of his work, and he had every right to be. It really was very creative and some of the pieces were very impressive and intricate.

Our family received a heartbreaking phone call one afternoon from New York City. Aunt Simonne shared that we had lost a Traveler; Uncle Arthur had passed away at the hotel that morning. My Uncle Alberic had watched him get up in the middle of the night, head towards the bathroom, and then return to bed after he was finished. The odd part was that Uncle Alberic claimed his brother was walking perfectly fine, without the use of his cane.

L to R - Top Row : My Aunt Simonne is the fourth in. Aunt Antoinette (Sister) is standing to the right of Simonne. L to R - Bottom Row : Third in is my Uncle Arthur, my grandmother Marie, my father Maurice with my Uncle Alberic at the end of the row.

A year later, in 1983, I was fifteen, and Sister again returned for a visit, concurrent with the first anniversary of Uncle Arthur's passing. My parents and I were invited to the apartment for a visit with Sister while she was home. My mother was not able to make the visit that night, as she was feeling under the weather, so it was going to be just my father and myself making the trip.

When Dad and I walked into the kitchen upon our arrival, a few of my aunts, including Simonne and Sister Antoinette, sat around the kitchen table near a window. On the opposite side of the kitchen sat Uncle Alberic in a rocking chair, warming himself by an ancient heater.

My dad sat at the kitchen table with my aunts, and I sat in a spare chair against the wall. The smell of cigarettes and a haze filled the room. The family was chatting in broken French and English. I always tried to figure out the conversations. They spoke solely in French when the topic was something they didn't want younger ears to understand. I did pick up on a lot of the conversations and learned some of the language over time, most of which I've long forgotten. However, I do remember most of the more colorful terms of language.

From my vantage point, I could see beyond the kitchen table to the bathroom door. To the right of that door was the long kitchen counter and sink with cupboards above. Straight ahead, at the end of the long counter, was my uncle Arthur's quiet bedroom. Walking straight from the kitchen into Arthur's room, his bed was still horizontally situated in his room. After about an hour or so, I started to develop a headache unlike any headache I'd ever had in my life. My head was in a vice, and my temples were being compressed like an orange in a juicer. I started to feel cold, yet warm and clammy, almost like a bad case of the flu - but I hadn't felt ill that day at all. My family's chatter at the kitchen table started to become muffled, and I started to experience some dizziness. I tried to act casual in an effort to keep myself together so no one would notice. In a last-ditch effort to maintain consciousness, I pulled my head up from my hands, only to witness the impossible.

Uncle Arthur walked out of his bedroom, along the path between the counter and table where everyone sat, still chatting up a storm. Dressed in his customary black pants with white undershirt, and walking with no cane, Uncle Arthur, looking straight ahead, just walked on by, never turning his head, never looking at any of us in the kitchen. He continued his trek right into the bathroom. Aside from being stunned and completely awestruck from what I just saw, I glanced at the faces of everyone in the room. Nobody broke conversation or turned to see him. Then I started freaking out on the inside. How was it possible nobody else was seeing what was going on here? Was I looking outwardly odd to my family? In complete disbelief, I became nauseous.

Will he be coming back out of the bathroom and when? I had some serious anxiety happening to me for a few minutes. Then it happened again. Uncle Arthur walked out, back across the kitchen, along the counters, and back into his bedroom. Putain de merde? It wasn't like he was an apparition; he was full-bodied and opaque. It was truly like he was in his bedroom being anti-social, and he needed to come out to use the restroom.

I started to have the chills and little tremors in my body. I presumed what I was feeling was shock and fear of the unknown. Just then, Aunt Simonne startled me back to this reality.

"Jéan, are you okay? What is wrong?" I certainly

couldn't tell her in front of everyone what I had just seen.

"I don't think I'm feeling well all of a sudden."

"Why don't you go lie down?" She suggested.

Frozen from fear, I uttered, "It will pass, I'll be okay," but I was working harder at convincing myself with my insistence rather than my aunt. Aunt Simonne stood, grabbed my hand, and started to escort me to the bedroom - Uncle Arthur's bedroom.

I immediately pulled back and said, "I'd rather sit out here with everyone." My aunt insisted I lie down and took me into the room. She turned off the light so it wouldn't bother my eyes or exacerbate my headache. Thank God the kitchen was all lit up and only a few feet away. I thought my head was going to explode because the pressure was so painful. I laid down on the bed, positioning myself sideways so my feet were still on the floor, and I looked out towards the kitchen.

"Why don't you lay on the bed correctly?"

"No, this is good." If I needed to make a quick exit from the room, I was ready to bolt and move as quickly as possible. I had, as you might imagine, an extremely uneasy feeling that I had never felt before. You know that feeling. It was like someone was staring at me, but I didn't know from where, and I was far too scared to even look. Slowly, I turned my head to the left, in the direction of Uncle Arthur's workshop. And there he was, standing in the doorway in a kind of light fog. Again, he was a solid figure.

Was he going to change into something scary? Something demonic or evil looking as seen in horror movies. My mind was racing. Even though Uncle Arthur was family, I was terrified. I mean, he always seemed angry when he was alive. I didn't want to imagine how he was going to be now. His face looked stoic with not a hint of emotion.

The stare between us felt like it lasted an hour, but in reality, it was probably five or ten seconds. Then the unthinkable happened, well, inconceivable in my mind. Uncle Arthur smiled at me. After all these years, he finally smiled, and it was just to me. No one in the kitchen could have seen him because of where he was in the room, not that they even saw him in the first place, as this all happened right in front of them. I'm pretty sure I cracked a little smile back to assure him that I saw his. Then he seemed to float straight backwards from the door through the fog. It was almost like he was on a slow airport moving walkway that was going backward. As his body backed away from the doorway, he started to disappear, and the workshop door closed slowly. Every ill feeling and anxiety I had dissipated. My headache, nausea, and chills faded. It was like a plug of energy and fear was just disconnected from an outlet. I rose from the bed and walked back into the kitchen, resuming my position in my original seat. Aunt Simonne asked if I was feeling better and I only nodded, yes.

After another hour or so, my father and I said our goodbyes for the night. My aunt, Sister, mentioned that she would drive to my house later in the week to visit with my mom. On the ride back home with my dad, I had to say something about seeing Uncle Arthur. My father, a devout Catholic, didn't believe in anything that he couldn't see, hear, or touch for himself. If there was no proof, then it didn't exist. I always found this to be contradictory. Isn't the Catholic faith about just that? Having faith because you ultimately have no physical proof? When I explained to him what had transpired for me that evening and why I felt ill, he only responded with a question.

"Are you doing drugs?" I kind of had an idea it may go that way.

"Of course, not!" I replied. He didn't believe a word I was telling him about seeing my dead uncle, and he insisted there had to be another explanation.

"Did you fall asleep in the chair and have a dream?"

"No!" I saw everyone in the kitchen and was wide awake, periodically coughing from all the cigarette smoke." I was certainly wide awake the whole time.

"Was it some kind of mirage or mind trick?"

"NO! Seriously?" I was actually pretty disappointed and a bit upset that my dad didn't believe me and he completely shrugged it off.

Once home, my mother asked how the night went, and I reluctantly told my story again, almost word-for-word what I had told my father. My mom smiled and said, "You know what, anything is possible." Well, I guess that was something, but it wasn't what I needed to calm my mind.

My Aunt : Sister Antoinette

A few days later when I returned home from school, my mom mentioned that The Travelers and Sister would be joining us for dinner on Saturday night. She suggested I tell my story to Sister to see what she thought. I waited in anticipation for Saturday to finally come. They arrived, and after a little time passed, I asked Sister if I could speak with her privately. She agreed, and we went into our den and closed the door. I explained in explicit detail the events that took place for me at the apartment on the night I saw Uncle Arthur. I remember her eyes grew a little wider as she listened intently to my story. When I finished, her first words made my jaw drop.

"I've seen him twice this past week because I'm staying in his old room."

I can't even explain how happy I was to know at that moment I wasn't crazy! All week I had been feeling afraid that maybe my dad was right.

"There's no such thing as ghosts. They don't exist," my father had said to me. "Once you die, that's it. Your last breath is your final existence on this planet and you turn to ash and bone. Once you're dead, Son, you're dead," he said to me.

I hated to go against my parents, but my mom always told me, "If you feel you're right, then stand up for yourself and fight until you prove your case. If we, as your parents, feel you are correct in your stance, we will back you, 100 percent. If not, you're on your own." She was a pretty tough and stubborn little Italian woman. She supported me on this, but my dad didn't. Sadly, I'd never be able to discuss this subject again with him because he's no longer with us. Funny thing is, he now knows there is something else after death.

Sister told me that she saw Uncle Arthur as she was turning in for the night. She was reading and put the book down to shut off the light. She glanced over to the workshop door and there was Arthur, looking back at her. They had not seen or talked to each other for years, and then he passed unexpectedly during that New York trip. I suppose he was coming to see her to say goodbye, and that's what she believed. He smiled at her like he had done to me and disappeared. The other sighting of Uncle Arthur was in the morning. Sister was walking out of the bedroom to go into the kitchen. She looked to her right, down the hallway, and saw Arthur from the back walking towards the parlor. He turned the corner into the parlor. She went down the hallway into the parlor, but he wasn't there. I finally felt my interaction with my deceased uncle had been confirmed. That conversation with my aunt, a Catholic nun, is the reason I believe in ghosts, the supernatural, and the paranormal - call it what you want. I figure there is no way that a Catholic nun is going to lie and make up false stories to make a young kid feel validated. If she witnessed what she said, then I know I saw what I did as well. After that night, as far as I know, Uncle Arthur hasn't been seen again. Most of the sixteen brothers and sisters have all passed. I have to believe they have all been reunited with their parents...if that's actually how it goes when you pass over to the other side.

CHAPTER 2

Tribal War Dance Warning

I started my sophomore year in high school - hanging around with most of the same kids I grew up with through the school system, and kids from my neighborhood. During school breaks, people would head out to the courtyard designated smoking area to huff on their cigarettes or play hackeysack. Hackeysack was the equivalent of a circle of people kicking a soccer ball between each other to keep it volleying in the air as long as possible, but with a beanbag. I played a few times but found it kind of boring, but I would hang out socializing with my friends. I didn't smoke either. It was just a time to get away from the teachers and school for ten to fifteen minutes. One morning, a friend of mine, Paul, asked if I heard about the big party on Saturday night. I said no, tell me about it. Paul said, "That newer kid, Dave, in our neighborhood is throwing a bash on Saturday night. His older brother is getting a keg and it should be fun. His parents will be out of town."

"Sounds like fun," I responded. Paul then started telling

me that he had heard from his older brother (who knew Dave's older brother) that their house was haunted. "Really?" I said with a bit of excitement.

"Apparently," Paul said, "They have heard strange chanting, and items have been moved or thrown from their regular resting places. Most of it originates in his parents' bedroom." Of course, I probably made a juvenile joke about his parents and their bedroom antics. Paul was serious about Dave's stories of the paranormal activity that was going on in their home.

I didn't know Dave well, just in passing in the school halls and he was in my gym class. He seemed like a normal kid that was pretty well put together and cool. Dave didn't seem too crazy or out of the ordinary any more than most of my friends back then. Saturday night came, and since his house was only a few streets away from mine, I walked over to his house. I got closer to the driveway and I was walking up to the house, I heard "Living after midnight" by Judas Priest rockin' in the night air. This kid had a band playing outside in his backyard. It was around 8pm when I got there. The party had started around 6pm, and there were a few kids that were pretty drunk already and more well on their way. I hung outside checking out the band for a few. They were playing mostly hard rock and heavy metal songs from Def Leppard, Aerosmith, Led Zeppelin, Black Sabbath and Van Halen. Well, they were trying hard, and for being teenagers, weren't horrible. I've heard worse, and I've actually played in worse bands in my very early days. There were a few kids chatting about the house being haunted. I asked what kind of hauntings or ghosts do they talk about? What is supposedly going on here? The rumor going around was that there was some kind of Native American spirit(s) haunting his house. Not long after the conversation started about what was apparently going on in Dave's house, he walked over to the group. We asked him to fill us in on this because most of us were interested. I was very interested because maybe only a year or two before this, I had seen my Uncle Arthur, so I was intrigued by ghosts and paranormal happenings.

Dave stated that his mother and father, on separate occasions, had heard what sounded like Native American Indians chanting, and faint sounds of tribal drums. Items on her bureau or night stand had been moved or actually thrown. This kid John pipes up and says, "There is no way, and no such thing as ghosts! I don't believe you." Dave then said, "Things don't seem to happen as often when my mom is alone, but when my dad is in the room alone, things happen all the time. He gets the feeling that whatever is there does not like men." John said, "I think this is all bullshit!"

Dave then said, "Go stay in the room for a while and see if something happens. If you can stay in there for two hours alone with the door shut, I'll give you $50.00."

"Deal," John said, "Easy money! Just give me a couple

beers and snacks and I'll be good to go." John hit the keg, grabbed two beers and went in the room. Then he came out and took a bowl of chips or pretzels off the kitchen table and went back into the room and closed the door. The first hour or so went by and John yelled from the room behind the closed door, "There's no one in here. You guys are so full of shit and I'm missing the party! If nothing happens in the next thirty minutes, I'm coming out!"

Dave said, "You agreed to two hours for fifty bucks. We'll still be partying all night."

"Fine!" said John, "I'll keep my end of the promise, but this is dumb!" About twenty minutes later, we hear John yell, "What the fuck!?" A few of us gathered by the bedroom door.

"What happened John?," somebody asked. We were talking through the door. John said, "Dave, your mother's perfume bottle just flew off the bureau onto the floor." Not long after, we started hearing things break – like breaking glass and loud thuds. We could hear this over the party and music. It was loud. John started yelling, "Some weird shit is happening! Things are flying around the room and pictures came of the wall, smashed and broke!" Dave said, "Are you messing with us and trashing my parents room to get back at us? Are you just pissed because you're missing the party and in the room, alone? If so, get out of the room and out of my house!"

"No, Dave!" John exclaimed, "Don't come in! I want to

see what will happen next." A few more minutes went by. All of a sudden, through the door, John yelled, "HOLY SHIT!!! I can hear drums and chanting, and it's getting louder and louder!" John wasn't exaggerating. By this point, the band outside had stopped playing. The word was going through the party guests about the dare between Dave and John. People started to gather in the living room which was across the hallway from the bedroom that John was in. We could hear low tribal drums and chanting through the door. Every few minutes we'd hear John saying things like, "OH MY GOD" or "HOLY SHIT!" What's going on now John, we'd say through the door. Everyone that was hanging around in the living room could hear the sounds coming from the bedroom, too. Half of us were intrigued while a few of the girls were getting scared. John yelled, "HE'S HERE!!! HOLY SHIT!!! HE'S HERE! DON'T OPEN THE DOOR!" The drums and chanting got louder behind the door so that there was no mistaking it. A bunch of us told John to just come out and stop breaking up Dave's parents' bedroom. John would reply saying he wasn't doing anything except laying on the bed. Everything going on in that room was happening around him. The chanting and drum sounds, at one point, seemed to be as loud as the band playing outside earlier. However, they weren't playing now because of the town's noise curfew of eleven o'clock. It was loud and we kept hearing things randomly breaking. There was a loud thumping sound that was different from the drum sound causing a vibration on the floor. We could feel it under our feet in the hallway.

"I'M DONE! I don't need fifty bucks that bad!" John yelled from the bedroom. Just then, the bedroom door flew open and John ran down the hallway and right out the backdoor. People were yelling, "John, wait!" He kept running down the driveway and up the street towards his house. He never said a word after the bedroom door opened, but when it did, a couple of us saw the apparition. It was a glowing Indian chief in full native regalia, full headdress and thumping the butt end of a long spear on the floor. He was full-bodied but a bit transparent. After a few seconds, he disappeared. The tribal drum sounds stopped and everything became calm again. When this was all going on, at the height of it, it sounded like an Indian Pow-Wow in full force. If you've been to one before, the comparison will make sense. Dave turned the light on and his parents' bedroom was completely trashed. Various items, like his mother's jewelry, photos, wall decor and end table lamps, were strewn about the room. There was broken glass from frames on the floor and on the bed. John only finished one beer. The other beer and bowl of snacks were thrown about the room. It looked like there was a food fight in the bedroom. I have to give it to John – he was a trooper to stay in there as long as he did. I probably wouldn't have, especially if there was going to be wasted alcohol. In our mid-teens, before we were able to drink legally, this would be considered alcohol abuse. We coveted any alcohol we could lay our hands on, so to see any wasted was a cardinal sin. Hindsight is twenty/twenty. When John was enduring the cranky Indian chief episode, I'm pretty sure none of us were worried about spilled beer.

On Monday morning, the school was buzzing about Dave's party and John's ghostly encounter. When I finally saw John in the school hallway, I told him, "Dude, a few of us saw the chief for a couple quick seconds before he disappeared. We know you weren't messing around." He replied, "I have never been so scared in my life! I saw him for a solid ten minutes. I was laying on the bed watching him slam his spear handle on the floor repeatedly. He was extremely angry and seemed to get angrier as time went on! He stared right through me as pictures were flying off the walls, and all kinds of things were being tossed around the room. I would keep hearing in my head, GET OUT! My body was paralyzed on the bed. I couldn't move! After a few minutes, I was finally able to get up and get out."

"That's some really scary and freaky shit!" I said. I ran into Dave later on in the day in the school cafeteria. I asked him if he was able to clean up his parents bedroom before they came home on Sunday. He said he tried to but his mom found stuff missing and in the wrong places. Plus all her pictures frames were broken. He had to fess up with his brother and take the hit for having the party. When he explained to his parents about the dare and John's encounter in the bedroom, they were extremely shocked. Dave was grounded for a month. Outside of school, I didn't see him around the neighborhood.

He came into school one day and told a bunch of us that his parents put their house up for sale. The reason was that his father was alone in the bedroom and the Indian chief appeared to him just as dramatically as he appeared to John. That was the final straw and they were moving. I never saw Dave again after he moved, but I can tell you, John became a believer of the supernatural.

He talked about the incident at Dave's house for the remaining years of our time in high school together and to anyone that would listen. It definitely scarred him and it was another huge eye-opener for me. While I had seen my Uncle in total solid human form, that Indian chief was a ghost. It was unlike anything, at that time, I had ever seen or witnessed in my life. To say that I and a few other kids that night were left unsettled and scared, would be an understatement. While this event didn't happen to me directly, and I'm glad it didn't, I did witness the Indian Chief and all that happened. That night was nothing short of mind-blowing, and was certainly a paranormal haunting that none of us could have envisioned.

CHAPTER 3

Are The Dead In The Living Room?

When I was sixteen, my parents separated and my mother moved out. My father and I lived together for the rest of my teenage years and into my twenties. Dad would frequently head to the aforementioned apartment in Lowell to hang out with his brother and sisters on the weekends. I always felt uneasy in my house alone, mostly in a couple specific places in the house.

Some families had that "special" living room that was off-limits - unless there were guests coming over. Our room had a sort of gaudy Italian look. My parents would entertain in this room every few months. There was nothing in that room but a couch, two chairs, a couple end tables and a stand-up, rarely played organ. Of course, there were wall hangings and decorative lamps with glass bases, along with some other accoutrements. Come to think of it, I'm not sure if the light bulbs were changed more than once every three years. The only time my parents and I used the room was at Christmastime, as it was where we decorated our tree. As in most traditional Cape Cod-style homes, the stairs to the second floor separated the living room from the dining room, another infrequently used room that only saw my family at Thanksgiving. Both of these rooms, positioned at the front of our house, were dark ninety percent of the time.

The room directly behind the wall of the living room was our TV room. This den is where my parents and I spent most of our leisure time. I would hang out there after school, watching cartoons, and later, in the early eighties, I would be rocking out every day with the newest music videos on MTV. Every time I would go into the den, I would walk by the living room just a little quicker. I immensely disliked the living room and the vibe emanating from it. At night, forget about it. I wouldn't even look into the room as I passed by. Whenever I would go upstairs to my room, I always went through the dining room from the kitchen, around the corner to the stairs. There was a railing that went up about five steps from which one could look over into the living room. Most times I never did and focused only upon going up the stairs. There was something about that room that just never sat well with me. It always felt as though someone was standing in the shadows, quietly watching your every move every day and night.

During my senior year of high school, I started dating this girl Katie. Since we were only a couple of months into our relationship, I would often travel to her house to pick her up for dates, or she would come and get me. Obviously, being teenagers, we went out a lot to avoid being stuck home with our parents.

At some point, my dad informed me he was going to Oklahoma for a week to visit one of his sisters. I thought this would work out perfectly, as I'd have the house to myself, and be able to be alone with my new girlfriend. On the evening of my father's departure, Katie came over after work. She had only briefly been in the house a few times, and usually only stepped into the kitchen when picking me up. After a quick, casual greeting and farewell to my dad, we departed for part of the evening. Katie and I returned after dinner to watch some TV, and I started to notice that every time she left the den, when she returned, she hurried by the living room doorway. Once I even caught her looking into the room, but she quickly turned away as she came back into the den.

"What's the matter?" I inquired, wondering if she was experiencing the same eeriness I had always felt.

"That room really creeps me out," she whispered, as if others could hear. I chose to say nothing, as it was a very new relationship, and I wasn't ready for any sort of awkwardness yet.

Another night during that week, Katie came over again; we made popcorn and watched a movie. Eventually, a sound emanated from the other side of the wall – from the living room. I paused the movie and listened.

Nothing.

I resumed the movie, but about ten minutes later, we heard the noise again. Once more, I paused the film to listen more carefully.

Again, there was nothing.

Figuring it was probably a noise from outside, we finished the movie. While the credits were rolling, we brought our popcorn bowls and trash into the kitchen. Katie walked out of the den into the hallway, heading toward the kitchen. Out of the corner of my eye, I saw her turn from looking into the dining room, and then she scrambled into the kitchen. Following her into the kitchen, I was almost afraid to ask what had happened.

"What was that all about?"

Katie hesitated, seemingly concerned about what my reaction might be if she answered honestly. "I saw a tall dark shadow standing in the room."

"Are you sure it wasn't your own shadow as you were walking by?"

"Definitely not," she replied more assertively.

Honestly, even though I had sensed some weirdness in that room for most of my life, I kind of blew it off, not thinking much of it. Within a few minutes after that, Katie and I said our good nights and she left.

As I walked through the dining room and climbed the staircase, I curiously glanced over the railing into the living room, and seeing nothing unusual, I continued on to bed.

The next morning, I went downstairs and noticed something a little odd. One of the old lamps on the end table was noticeably moved. After my mom left, my father and I didn't use that room at all, and only for very occasional dusting did we move anything. Alright, maybe a bit less than occasionally. Nevertheless, it looked as if the lamp had slid a couple of inches sideways, leaving a cylindrical clean spot on the table where it had been. I thought that was extremely odd and I left it that way; I was curious to see if it would move again. Each day afterward, I checked for any changes, but there were none. Eventually, I forgot about it.

On Friday night of that week, Katie was coming over to stay the night. We ordered a pizza delivery and rented a movie. As the night went on, everything seemed pretty normal. The couch in the den pulled out into a sleeper, so we decided to hang out in the den, watch television, and ultimately sleep there for the night.

At some point in the middle of the night, Katie awoke to get a drink of water and use the bathroom, which was right across the hall from the living room. Still asleep, I was immediately awakened when I heard a scream. I furiously jumped up from the couch to see what happened.

"What's the matter I asked?"

Katie was visibly frightened. "The big shadow – I saw it! In the living room by the front picture window."

"It must have been your own shadow; the moon shines

through that window," I tried to console her.

"It wasn't me!" Katie was adamant. "This time, the figure was half shadow and half man, a taller man!"

"What was he wearing?" I asked with honest curiosity.

"It happened so fast, I don't even know," she responded in complete bewilderment.

At first, I thought she might have been messing with me, but then I recalled the positioning of the lamp from earlier in the week. Where she saw the man would have been next to the end table with the lamp. I felt a familiar anxiety begin to rise within me, however, for Katie's peace of mind, I kind of played it off as nothing.

"It was probably nothing - or maybe just some kind of weird light anomaly. I'm sure everything is fine," I told her, but I realized the stark truth: I was trying to convince us both.

Katie left early that Saturday morning, and my father arrived home from his trip later that afternoon. He and I talked about Oklahoma and the activities he did with my aunt and uncle while there. That evening Katie called, inviting me out for dinner. She picked me up later that evening for our date, and when we returned to my house later, she parked her car, curbside, in front of my house.

After chatting together for a while in the darkness, Katie said, "I think your dad is looking out the window at us."

"He probably can't see that it's your car and that it's us." We weren't by the street light, so it was pretty dark, and the kitchen light was the only light emanating from the house.

About twenty minutes later Katie said, "There he is again!" I turned and looked toward the house. Back-lit from the kitchen light, I saw the shadow of a head and shoulders peering out the window.

"I'd better go in because he's probably getting nervous that someone may be casing our house or something," I told Katie. I kissed her goodnight, exited the car, walked across the front lawn, and made my way up the short walkway to the back door, the entryway into our kitchen. I walked in, expecting to find my dad either in the kitchen or the den watching TV, but the kitchen was empty and the den was in darkness.

"Dad?" I called to him, but there was no answer.

I walked through the dining room to the bottom of the stairs. It was then that I heard a noise coming from his bedroom at the top of the stairs. I started walking upstairs, and half way up I recognized the noise. I peeked into the room, and my father was deeply sleeping and snoring loudly.

"Who was in the window? I immediately thought. There was nobody else it could be. It only took approximately three minutes to walk from the car to the bottom of the stairs. There was absolutely no way he could have gone upstairs and fallen asleep that quickly; it was impossible.

The next morning, I awoke to my dad calling me from the bottom of the stairs. He had already been up for a bit. I rolled out of bed and went to the top of the stairs to see what he wanted. He asked me, "Why did you empty my coffee out into the sink?"

"Huh? What do you mean?" I asked. I joined him downstairs and told him I hadn't been out of bed yet – that he had just woken me up.

"I was in the bathroom shaving, and I heard footsteps and noise from the kitchen, so I thought you were up," he clarified.

Apparently, my dad had poured his coffee into a mug and left it on the counter to cool a bit while he was shaving. When he returned to it, he found the coffee poured into the sink and the mug still on the counter.

Taken aback by this revelation, I said, "Dad, that was not me!" He looked at me like I had three heads. But this immediately reminded me of the previous evening's scenario.

"Hey, Dad, what time did you go to bed last night.?"

"Around eleven, why?"

I had come in the house around 1am.

I proceeded to tell him about the shadow figure in the window. Similar to how I had handled Katie's sighting, my dad brushed off the story. He didn't believe me - again.

"Then explain your coffee and the noise in the kitchen?" I implored.

My father paused for a moment as if to speak, but then quietly walked away. No explanation. No rebuttal. Nothing. I don't think he was convinced that something strange was going on. I just think he didn't want to discuss what he thought was nonsense, and he wanted to get on with his day.

Smokey and the Bandit was on TV the following Saturday night, and I loved that movie. Burt Reynolds was so cool, and the Trans Am he sped around in was even cooler.

The Trans Am used in Smokey And The Bandit 2 movie

I decided to stay home alone, and watch it in my room. Walking into my uncommonly large adolescent bedroom, my bed was along the left wall. My TV and my stereo were on the top of the dresser situated at the foot of my bed. The TV illuminated my room with the sounds of screeching tires, and "I'll get you, you sumbitch!" coming from my stereo speakers. Completely engrossed in Bandit's antics, out of the corner of my eye I saw something passing by the side of my head. Figuring I imagined it, I ignored it and continued watching The Bandit outwit and out-drive

Officer Buford T. Justice.

At a commercial break, I decided to run downstairs for a drink and snack before the movie resumed. I stepped into the dark hallway, barely lit by the flicker of the TV. Immediately, there was a cracking sound from under my foot. I had stepped on my Dokken "Under Lock And Key" cassette and completely crushed the case. Shards of plastic strewn across the hallway floor, I undeniably know that tape was not there when I entered my bedroom. Then it struck me; that cassette was on my dresser next to the TV. Was that what had flown by my head in the dark a little while before?

In the morning, I again attempted to speak with my father about all of the weird occurrences from the previous days.

"There has to be a reasonable explanation," he stated, his response an echo from when I had seen my uncle. I walked away feeling defeated. Not only couldn't I open his eyes, but I also couldn't even pique his interest about the possibility that more than just the two of us were in the house.

What was going on? Who was this being? What did he, she, or it want? Was it only one entity – or many? At least when I saw my Uncle Arthur, I knew exactly who he was, but these experiences were very different. I had no idea about anything, and it made me feel uneasy. You know the adage "what you don't know can't hurt you?" I can tell you, unequivocally, that's not completely true, and I eventually discovered that a few years later.

Chapter 4
Blood Cemetery

In New Hampshire during the mid-eighties, the back roads of a small town called Hollis used to be the best escape routes from major roads to avoid any chance of encountering police, especially if you had been partying. Beyond the farms and fields, tucked away in a secluded, sleepy forest, there is a dark and quiet cemetery. Its official name is "Pine Hill Cemetery," but most locals know it as "Blood Cemetery," as one of the first families to be buried there in 1730 were members of a local family named Blood. Rumors abound about the fate of multiple family members from the Blood clan, but the predominant belief is the family had been murdered. The headstones of Abel and Sarah Blood, along with those of some of their relatives, face a dirt path in the center of the cemetery. Visitors must hike up a long, steep hill to the top to view most of the older graves. It always looks very eerie at night when the light of the moon casts its glow over the grounds. There are still no street lights on these dark back roads. The cemetery is heavily patrolled at night, and a hefty fine is issued to anybody caught trespassing after dusk.

I used to drive past Blood Cemetery frequently, and I always developed an uneasy feeling in the pit of my stomach. There were all sorts of local legends about the cemetery and its weird happenings. Most stories were pretty wild and not very believable. I had never personally gone into the cemetery, but I did always harbor a slight curiosity about seeing some of the anomalies described by others. Was there any truth to the stories, or were they just that, fabricated stories?

One July night, Katie and I were driving through Hollis, and I knew we were going to pass Blood Cemetery. She wasn't a fan of the place either, so I would mess with her whenever we drove by. "We should go in because who's going to bother you? They're dead! Maybe the curse of Able Blood is true and he's going to get you." I personally thought all or most of the stories were fake. On this warm summer night, we headed into Hollis to hang out with some friends. As we drove past the cemetery, I yelled at the top of my lungs out the window towards the graves.

"Wake up, Dead! W A K E U P!!"

Katie freaked out. "Don't do that! Are you nuts?"

"You're such a wuss," I laughed.

"I am not!" she vehemently opposed.

A few hours later, Katie and I left our friend's gathering and headed back to Katie's house, needing to pass

Blood Cemetery again. I figured I'd continue my quest to scare Katie, but the joke was ultimately on me. As we approached the property, I again yelled out the window, "WAKE UP, DEAD!" Then the strangest thing happened. It was like the sky opened up over my car for the twenty-five yard stretch of road in front of the cemetery, and we were pelted with tiny objects. It was as if 3,000 bouncing super balls dropped from the sky. The weirdest thing.

"I told you! You shouldn't have done that!" Katie yelled, scolding me.

No lie, I was stunned and a bit shaken by this, and I sped up. After passing the cemetery, the barrage stopped. It only lasted about five seconds, but that was long enough.

"We have to go back tomorrow, during the day," I implored. "I have to see if there are trees hanging over the roadway, or just try to find some explanation." Katie was silent.

The next morning, Katie and I returned to investigate, searching for any kind of debris or a sign of what the objects could have been. Acorns from overhanging tree limbs was certainly my initial thought. We arrived, looked around, and saw nothing on the ground or by the road's sides. There were no tree branches looming over the road either, just clear, blue sky overhead. Convinced we would find the source of the noise, I became frustrated by the incessant questions multiplying in my brain, and the diminishing possible answers. By that afternoon, I was more confused than I had been when it actually happened. What had hit my car?

Although it was a pleasantly warm day, at one point I felt very cold, almost as if I had walked into a meat cooler for a moment. I took Katie's hand in mine, and ambled speculatively down the cemetery's pathway toward the road. By the time we had reached my parked car on the roadside, I was riddled with an overwhelming sensation of guilt. I unlocked the passenger door, opening it for Katie, who made herself comfortable and who was visibly relieved that we would be leaving momentarily. Closing her door, I turned toward the cemetery again, and I could not help myself.

"I'm sorry to have been disrespectful by yelling and bothering your rest. Please forgive me." My impromptu utterance surprised me. I paused for another few seconds, holding a stare with the hallowed property, as if hoping to receive some sort of atonement. But, rankly abused by myself and many others over the years, I could feel it glaring back at me, with no martyr-ish offerings of forgiveness in sight.

When I entered work the next day, I told the story to my co-worker, Debbie, who was extremely interested in the paranormal. She told me a story about when she lived in Ireland. She used to traverse the country trying to find the markers of deceased people that were thought to have been evil or considered witches. Deb explained that markers are all around the Irish countryside where pieces of bodies are buried. Bodies of suspected witches or evil-doers used to be quartered, and the pieces buried in the north, south, east and west so bodies could not be reassembled. A stone with the information of the person was erected where the head was buried. I thought this was a pretty extreme practice, but apparently, back then, the Irish deemed it a necessity.

"Dude! Take me there! I want to check this place out – and any other creepy cemeteries around here – let's do some ghost-hunting!" Reluctant from my experience the previous day, after she kept hounding me, I eventually agreed.

Let me tell you, I couldn't wait to tell Katie that we were going back to Blood Cemetery, and now... going in. I knew she'd flip out. She was completely against it, and wanted nothing to do with this new adventure. To be perfectly honest, I wasn't too thrilled about it either, but I played it off as no big deal – come to think of it, I was pretty dismissive about it. I was a guy, a tough teenager, and, c'mon, I couldn't show any fear or weakness.

The following weekend Katie, Deb, myself, and a couple others from work took the ride up to the cemetery. It was about ten o'clock at night, and the moon, high in the sable sky, brightly illuminated the night. Katie, appalled by the decision to return, refused to exit the car. We grabbed our flashlights and began walking up the steep dirt path to the top of the hill. The cemetery is embraced by a short, four-foot stone wall. Reaching the crest of the hill, I saw Abel Blood's headstone. These are older stones from the 1600's to 1800's. A lot of the stones have broken or been vandalized over the years. Some have been cemented back together.

The group of us went our separate ways to investigate. On Abel's stone, I noticed there was a hand on it. One fairly "well-documented" story is that the hand on Abel Blood's stone reverses direction at night. The hand, pointing to the heavens, is said to reverse and point to hell at night. People have claimed that blood has seeped out of the headstone and covered the hand as well. That is one of the stories I feel is exaggerated. I can say the hand was upright and its finger was pointing toward the sky when I was there that night.

Abel Blood Sr. tombstone.

Then, all of a sudden, there was a sound of what seemed like a metallic ding. It sounded like a quarter striking a mailbox is how I can best describe it. I thought one of the people whom we were with was pranking us somehow. Keep in mind, Katie was still in the car. Frantically all the different beams from the flashlights start moving quickly toward the main dirt path where I was standing.

Everyone babbled at once, "Did you guys hear that?" and "What was that noise?"

"Which of you guys did that?"

Everyone said it wasn't them and they thought maybe I was the prankster. I swore it wasn't me, and it wasn't. Just then, that same metallic sound rang out again, but this time it was a little louder, seemingly closer to us. We were all standing close together, so it was obvious it wasn't any of us making those sounds.

"Stay together," I warned everyone, and I proceeded to climb the hill to walk the perimeter of the cemetery along its rock wall, looking for anything or anyone that could have made the noise we heard. There was nothing, no one. The sylvan cemetery has no neighboring houses. No one knew we were there, and as a matter of fact, not one car passed on the road either. It was late, and that road at night is not heavily traveled. I headed back to meet my friends and told them I found nothing. Someone suggested we leave, so we headed down the dirt path back to the car.

Discussing where to go next, we stopped in our tracks. BANG! That metallic sound crashed loudly right behind us. It was as if someone had slammed two metal trash can lids together. Obviously startled, I glanced behind me as I immediately started running. No one was there. I turned to see my friends, already halfway down the path, scrambling to the car as if they were being chased by a street gang. Finally reaching the car and completely out of breath, I jumped in the driver's seat, started the engine, and peeled out of there. Everyone was panting and scared.

As we calmed down and headed back to civilization, Katie finally spoke up. "Who was the other person up there with you guys?" she asked.

"What do you mean?" I countered her.

"When you were coming back down the path I could see your silhouettes back-lit from the moon and the flashlights in your hands, but there was one more person."

"What do you mean?" I repeated.

"The person...on the path...right behind you – who was it?"

"Katie," I said firmly, "there was nobody else up there except for the four of us."

"No, there was someone else. They didn't have a flashlight, but they were holding up something shiny – I could see the moonlight reflecting off it when they raised it up."

"What are you talking about?!" I seriously thought she was hallucinating.

"I could see you, and I counted four flashlights coming down the path. I wanted to make sure you were still all together. But I am telling you, there were four flashlights and five people." Katie glared at me, set her jaw, and folded her arms; she spurned any idea remotely contrary to what she claimed she had seen.

Paranormal adrenaline junkies that we were, we then visited a couple of other cemeteries in the area, however, no incidents occurred like that which happened at Pine Hill Cemetery. All night, I couldn't help but wonder, and continually ask myself what did Katie see? Who else could have been there with us? We neither saw anyone around nor even heard the sounds of animals rustling in the woods.

The following day Katie came to pick me up for a lunch

date. Completely preoccupied, I told her we have to go back to Blood Cemetery. "We need see if we can figure this out or at least find any metallic objects that could have made the sound we all heard."

"Not a chance," she uttered, but she eventually gave in.

"C'mon, it's daytime and we'll be fine. We won't stay long - we can just take a quick look around," I convinced her. We proceeded through the gate and walked along the rock wall around the perimeter of the cemetery. We didn't see anything made of metal, not even an empty can or bottle cap. As we started strolling down the dirt path, I noticed something odd. There was a pretty good sized, half- buried rock in the dirt. The odd part was there was a white scrape on the side of the rock, like something sharp had forcefully hit it. It dawned on me and I realized this was about the spot I was at while on the path walking back to the car when we heard the loud bang. There was a four to five inch straight deep divot in the dirt next the rock. It clearly resembled the mark of an ax.

"Oh, my God," I said under my breath. Is it possible that the shiny glimmer Katie saw of the figure behind me was the blade of an ax raised in the air? Certain points started adding up from what I witnessed that night and what she saw, but couldn't hear from inside the car. I grabbed her hand.

"Let's go," I said, "there's nothing more to see in here."

As Katie and I walked back to her car, I couldn't help

thinking about that sound and replaying the events of the previous night in my head. That loud noise definitely could have been the sound of metal hitting stone extremely hard ... I know there was no one else up there that night but the four of us ... I didn't witness the figure Katie had seen where I had heard the strange noise, the same spot where I had stood the previous night, the same spot where we saw the scraped rock.

What was out there with us? Was someone that resides in the cemetery retaliating for my yelling, "Wake up, Dead" as we had previously driven by? Was I targeted, or was this just a separate incident in a known-to-be-haunted cemetery? I'll never know. I can say these two experiences have stayed with me for over thirty five years, and when I think about that night, I still have a multitude of questions about how, what, and why.

I returned to that cemetery once more, about twenty-five years ago, with my wife Kerry. I had told her this story, and she wanted to check out the cemetery for herself. While nothing happened to us during our daylit visit, I still felt very uneasy all over again; I felt unwelcomed, and rightfully so I suppose. I didn't have any reason to be there again or ever, for that matter. Some of the published stories from other visitors that I've read may, in fact, be true. Still, while many may be embellished, who am I to judge or comment on the experiences of others, especially in a place so notably tenebrous. Occasionally, I drive by the cemetery when I have to, and each time, I am still haunted by the memory of that enigmatic night all those years ago.

I recently returned to the cemetery on October 6th, 2024 to take the photo below and see if the cemetery still looks the same. The original dirt path leading up to the top of the hill where the Blood family graves were is now all grass. The entrance and path leading to the top of the hill has been moved to the far left of the cemetery. Sadly, most of the tombstones have been desecrated, or removed completely. Abel Blood Sr., Abel Blood Jr., Willard Blood and Betsy's stones have been removed altogether. Abel Blood Sr's wife Sarah's stone can be seen in the photo below. It has been broken in two and is now laying in the grass. I find it extremely shameful and disgusting the way some people disrespect the dead. Ghost hunting and exploring is one thing, vandalism is simply wrong.

Sarah Blood's broken tombstone. The open area to the left of these stones are where all the other family stones were. Photo taken on 10/6/24.

Pine Hill Cemetery (Blood Cemetery) is considered one of the spookiest and most haunted places in New Hampshire. During the few times I was there, I don't think it was as well documented as it is today. For me, it was hearing second – and third – hand stories that piqued my interest. Many ghost hunting and paranormal investigations have been conducted there, which a quick Google search can confirm, and I'm sure other interesting accounts have been added over the years. Which stories from "Blood Cemetery" will you believe?

Chapter 5

What's A Ouija Board?

I t was a frigid winter's Saturday night in 1987, everything outside was cold, dark, and silent. Home alone for the weekend, I was bored and indecisive about what to do, if anything. I guess going to a club or seeing a local friend's band was an option, but I really despise being cold. Really, I had no interest in venturing away from the warmth of home. I played my guitar to some KISS records for a while, but that got old after an hour or so. Eventually, I made some phone calls to friends in an effort to create a little get-together. Much like myself, no one was interested in venturing out into the bitter cold weather, until I reached Chris.

Chris was a guy with whom I became friends through work. He was into music, sci-fi, and drama - not causing it, although that did happen on occasion, but more like acting in and filming his own VHS videos. I think he wanted to be a director of sorts. He was extremely quirky, but fun to hang with.

"I just got a Ouija Board game for Christmas. I could

come over and we could mess around with it and see if it works," Chris offered.

"What's a Ouija Board game?" I asked.

"It's supposedly a way to contact dead people and spirits. Apparently, you can get answers to questions about whatever you want to ask." This really intrigued me.

"You mean I could potentially talk to my deceased rock heroes - like Randy Rhoads and John Bonham?"

"Yeah, if you want, and if they come through."

"Okay, bring it over and let's give it a go." I figured, worst case scenario, nothing happens and I kill a night of adolescent boredom.

Chris showed up and we immediately got down to business with the Ouija Board. While I already believed in ghosts, I kind of thought this whole concept was silly - ghostly entertainment from Parker Brothers (a huge game company at the time). Was this thing really going to work, or was it all just ... "entertainment?"

The two of us sat on the floor upstairs in my bedroom. With both of us placing our index fingers on the game's planchette, we started asking questions. For anyone unfamiliar with Ouija, the planchette is a pointed piece with a window cut out of the middle to easily read the letters or words on the board. It can also hover over a letter so it appears in the hole cutout. Then if it moves it spells out words or can point to "yes" or "no" on the board answering your questions. "Goodbye" is also listed as an option on the board when you're doing your ghostly conversation. We never got to "Goodbye."

We started out with "Is anyone here with us?" Nothing happened.

"Is anyone going to move this thing?" We did this for about ten minutes and nothing happened.

"Dude," I said, "I think this is a waste of time and a joke."

Chris persisted, "Let's try it again for a few more minutes."

"Okay, fine!"

A short time later, we put our fingers back on the planchette and I said, "Is Randy Rhoads here?" For those that may not know, Randy Rhoads was Ozzy Osbourne's guitarist, killed in a tragic plane crash while the band was on tour. Anyway...Nothing! No movement. Why would Ozzy Osbourne's deceased guitarist be in my bedroom anyway? I felt like we were being idiots, wishing for some kind of spiritual fun to magically happen.

So, prepared to give up, I asked again, "Is there anyone here with us?" The planchette moved slightly. "Chris, why are you moving it?"

"I'm not!"

I thought he was messing with me, but intrigued, I continued.

"If there is someone here with us, say yes!" The planchette moved and pointed to "Yes." We began asking basic questions to this "possible" spirit: How old are you? When did you die? How did you die?

Then I said, "Make something move in my room or do something to prove you're real so I know that Chris isn't moving the planchette." Here's where the night started getting strange.

As I previously mentioned, it was obnoxiously cold outside and I hate being cold, so I had the thermostat in the house set to around seventy degrees. After about an hour, I made a comment to Chris that it was starting to get really warm in my room. I figured, because we were sitting on the floor, the heat from the baseboard registers were directly heating us up. We continued to ask simple questions like, are you a man? Are you a woman? Where are you from? Easy questions like that. I honestly don't remember the responses, but I do, in fact, remember certain aspects about this experience I will never forget.

Chris and I quickly fell deeper into this conversation with the Ouija Board, and at some point we realized hours had passed since we had begun. I started sweating uncomfortably and announced, "I'm going to run downstairs to turn the heat down a little."

When I reached the thermostat, the dial was pegged past ninety degrees. There was nothing digital. To turn the temperature up or down, someone had to manually rotate the dial. How in the world did that dial spin past ninety degrees? Chris hadn't left my room since his arrival earlier that evening. As a matter of fact, neither of us had even walked past the thermostat at all; I was the last person to set the temperature, and that was earlier in the day. I returned upstairs and told Chris what I had found. He had this blank look on his face like he had seen a ghost.

"Can you believe that?" I asked Chris. He shrugged, but I immediately resumed my questions again.

"Did you turn the heat up?"

The planchette moved to "Yes."

"Who are you?" we asked.

The point on the planchette made its way around the board and spelled out "Dead."

"No kidding, you're dead? Can you be a little more specific Mr. or Mrs. Ghost?" I just wanted specific answers to my questions. Was that too much to ask? We blurted out a few more questions and that planchette was zipping around the board pretty quickly. It seemed to have a lot of power and/or energy.

"Do something again if you truly turned the heat up. Make something move and prove to me you're real." I was antagonizing this spirit-so-to-speak because I was still kind of skeptical about this whole Ouija Board game. I needed proof, and I wanted answers.

Chris and I started becoming almost addicted to the game. It was odd. It was the curiosity factor of what would come next. What would it say? What would it do? We actually felt like we couldn't stop or take a break. What if the ghost went away? What if we got a boring ghost that doesn't like chatting? What if John Bonham came through and would explain how he does those amazing triplets in "Good Times, Bad Times" with one foot? (Bonham, who passed away in 1980, was the drummer for the seventies super group Led Zeppelin).

Still uncertain as to what might be happening at that moment, I was certain it was either unbelievably amazing or completely dumb. The spirit still had yet to say who it was, but I had a pretty good feeling it wasn't any of the rock n' roll legends whom I had called upon earlier.

I realized at one point my teeth were chattering a little bit and I was getting cold chills. "Chris, I'm going back downstairs to turn the heat back up a bit.

I may have turned it down too much when it was jacked up off the scale earlier," I admitted. I headed down the stairs and over to the thermostat again.

"Are you kidding me?" I said aloud.

The dial was turned all the way down, past fifty degrees. It was so cold in the house; it felt like it was in the forties in the kitchen. I ran back upstairs and again told Chris what I found. He had that blank stare look again. I again asked him, "Can you even believe this?"

"Yes - I can! That planchette just moved by itself. I heard you say something downstairs, and it moved to 'Yes.'"

"Get out of here!" I exclaimed

"Dude, I'm serious!" Chris assured me. "What did you

say when you were downstairs? I heard you speaking, but couldn't make out the words."

I told him I had said, "Are you kidding me?" Apparently, our ghostly companion in the room had answered me. Well, now I was adamant about knowing more from this entity.

I asked, "Did you turn the heat completely off?"

The planchette moved to "Yes."

So let me ask you this, "Can you see the future?"

The answer was "Yes."

"Am I going to get married?"

It moved to "Yes" again. Back then, I thought there was no way I'd ever get married, but currently I am and have been for thirty years.

"Will I have any kids?" No movement of the planchette.

"Am I going to be a famous rock star like my idols in the posters on my wall?" The answer was "Yes."

I then asked, "When will I die?"

It pointed to the number five, then the number four.

Stunned, I asked again, "You're saying I'm going to die when I'm fifty-four?"

It went back and pointed to the number five and the number six.

I inquired further, "So you're saying I'm going to die at fifty-four or fifty-six?" The planchette was still for a moment and then raced shot over to "YES." It moved with such force that our fingers could barely stay on it.

I'll admit, after that I was feeling a little uneasy. Who was telling me this? Was it a family member, or someone whom I knew that had passed? I was only twenty years old at this point, so I hadn't really lost many people in my life yet. Frustrated, I angrily and sternly shouted out "WHO ARE YOU?"

The planchette moved over "E." Then it moved to the letter "V." Next was "I."

Chris and I both took our fingers off the planchette, as we had an idea what the next letter might be. We looked at each other in amazement and fear.

"I think you've been moving the playing piece, the planchette. I think you've been messing with me all night," I announced to Chris, knowing full-well he couldn't have.

Chris half-chuckled in his own disbelief at what had unfolded, and repeated that he definitely had nothing to do with any of the board's responses.

"If it was me, then who messed with the thermostat?"

Okay, he had a good point. He never left my room from the time he walked in the door. I looked at the clock and it was close to 4am. Chris had arrived about 8:30pm.

Shocked at the hours that had passed, I announced, "Well, time to pack it up."

As we turned to put the board back in the box, the planchette moved by itself very slowly to the letter "L." Then we both started freaking out.

"Get that thing out of my house and don't ever bring it

back!" I yelled.

We quickly slammed the board and its planchette back into the box. Then Chris said his goodbyes and split. I don't think I went to sleep until I saw the sun starting to rise. I was really freaked out by the entire night.

To this day, I still worry at times about the age of my demise. A few of the questions that Chris and I asked that frigid night came to fruition: I am married, I didn't have a child of my own. Kerry and I came close a few times, but my life's direction didn't allow us to have children for whatever reasons. I've made half a living being a musician and touring, performing for thousands of people. I guess the spirit was half correct. A rock star and known by many, I guess. People call me that. Famous? Not in the least. I don't consider myself a rock star. I just think of myself as a guy who loves to rock and I have been doing it pretty well for over forty years. Now, as I close this chapter, I'm fifty-five years old and my birthday is quickly approaching. For so long I felt compelled to write this book because - what if the "evil spirit" was correct about my passing at the age of fifty-six? I sure hope not, but if this ends up being my only book, you'll know why.

My rock n' roll self in 1987

CHAPTER 6

Who Are You All And Why Are You Here?

In the winter of 1992, December 4th to be exact, Kerry moved into the house with me and my dad. She brought with her a couple cats and one dog. By this time my father had moved his bedroom downstairs for convenience and Kerry and I would take the master bedroom which was my parents' former bedroom on the second floor. Not very long after Kerry was with us, she started sensing strange things were happening. She'd see light anomalies and orbs in the bedroom and around the upstairs. I used to tell her she was seeing things and it was probably car headlights from the next street over coming through the window. That did happen often and was an obvious explanation to extra light in the room. However, I will now admit I would see little orb lights coming out of the closet in the bedroom or from the hallway into the bedroom as well. I certainly didn't want Kerry to be nervous and move out as fast as she moved in. We had been dating since June of 1992 and I was falling for her pretty hard.

Strap yourselves in for this one as this was the most intense paranormal experience we both had encountered. One night when we were going to sleep, we shut the TV off, kissed goodnight and rolled over for the night. I remembered having really odd dreams of people I had never seen, met or known. They just randomly popped into my dreams and I'd awake with confusion. Like I mentioned earlier, I could go for months without remembering a dream. To this day, it still happens. I don't think I've remembered any dream for at least four or five months, yet you apparently dream every night. That's what "they" say.

The dream started with a woman and a young boy. She was probably in her late twenties to early thirties. The boy was about seven or eight years old.

They were walking around what seemed to be a farmhouse with a lot of land around it outside. Doing farming-type chores is what it seemed.

Then... I'd wake up! Who are these people? I couldn't figure it out.

Kerry kept telling me there's someone or something here in the room. On occasion we'd argue about it and agree to disagree. Well, I did but she was more adamant about her feelings and thoughts. One day after work I was in the shower and one of the shampoo bottles came flying off the back shelf where we would keep everything. It flew off with such force and hit me in the upper area of my leg. It missed the family jewels by inches. I actually let out a loud "OWWWW" and a couple expletives. I was stunned! Kerry came into the bathroom to see what happened and if I was OK. I told her, "The shampoo bottle just came flying at me and hit me in the leg. I didn't see it coming because I was rinsing my hair and had my eyes closed."

"Maybe it fell off the shelf!" she exclaimed.

"No way!" I stated, "If it had just fallen off the shelf it would have fell into the tub, not hit me in my upper leg."

Perplexed, I finished my shower and got out quickly. We tried to recreate the bottle falling but to no avail. Nothing matched up. It was thrown at me with force and intent. Intent to hurt me, get my attention or what? No doubt it was thrown.

Not long after, I got a pretty good black and blue bruise on my leg. This same incident continued happening every third or fourth time I'd be in the shower.

Kerry said "We should get a Ouija board and try and see if we can figure out who you're seeing in your dreams."

"NOPE!" I said. "I've already had a bad experience with a Ouija board, and how do you know about Ouija boards?"

She said, "My grandmother used to use them a lot when I was young. She also used to read tarot cards and was into the supernatural. She tried to teach me but I was young, but the whole thing is fascinating to me and I have her Ouija boards." I reluctantly agreed to use the board and see what, if anything, would happen. We picked a Saturday afternoon when my dad was away to give it a shot, figuring it was during the day and nothing ghostly happens during daylight hours. Kerry lit a candle and we sat in the upstairs bathroom before we started. Our boxer dog "Bronson" continued to come into the bathroom, interrupting us. We closed the door and of course he started scratching at the door to come in. I suggested I take him to the basement while we do this and bring him up when we're done. I didn't have my music studio down there yet, so I brought Bronson into the basement and clipped his collar to a tie out cable that was around one of the main support poles. I went back upstairs to the second floor bathroom where Kerry was waiting for me to continue the Ouija board quest.

We asked the same typical questions : "Is there anyone here with us? Please talk to us."

The planchette started moving right away. Kerry swore she wasn't moving it and neither was I.

"Who are you?" We asked. The planchette spelled out "Anna." "What's your full name?" I asked. It spelled Anna M. Ok, I'm thinking we're getting somewhere. Kerry was smart and brought in a pad of paper and took notes of the specific answers we were getting. "Are you the only person here with us?" I asked. "No," Anna said. "How many?" I questioned. "Many," Anna showed as an answer on the board. "Do you throw the shampoo bottle at me when I'm in the shower?" I asked her. Her reply was "NO!" "Well then who is doing that?" I asked again. "Him," she said. So I'm thinking, well that's not very helpful.

"What are you doing here and what do you want?" I asked. Her reply was "son."

"You want your son?" I said. "YES" is where the planchette went to on the board.

I asked Anna, "Is your son the one throwing the shampoo bottle at me?"

"NO!" she replied. Are you kidding me? So now we have a lady looking for her son, and "Him."

I looked at Kerry and said, "Who are all these people?" She replied with, "How am I supposed to know. I just recently moved in." Okay, well she had a point and it was really a rhetorical question anyway. We continued asking many questions and Kerry kept jotting down the info.

Then out of nowhere there was scratching on the bathroom door. We both looked at each other with bewilderment and probably a little fear. We were the only ones home and the dog was in the basement. "It's got to be one of the cats," I said. I opened the door and there's "Bronson" sitting in the hallway. OK, this is completely INSANE! I clipped his leash to his collar and had the cellar door closed. How is this even possible? Kerry said, "Maybe you thought you clipped him to his collar and didn't shut the basement door tight?" Is it a possibility? Sure, it's got to be something like that. That seems like a reasonable explanation. "I'll go put him back in the basement and

double-check everything this time." Bronson and I proceeded back down the two flights of stairs to the basement.
I clipped his long leash to his collar again. Double-checked
it. It's on and secure. Went back up the basement steps and
closed the door. Gave the door a tug and yes, it's shut tight.
Back upstairs to the bathroom I go.

I sat back down with Kerry and we start the Ouija pro-
ceedings again. "Anna, are you still here?" We asked.

"YES," she replied.

"What's your full name?" we asked again. "Anna Marie"
it spelled. "What's your son's name?" we asked.

"Alexander," she said.

"Okay, so who is 'Him'?" There was no reply or answer
given. I asked, "Is 'Him' your husband?"

"NO," she responded. I figured if her son was here
maybe her husband was too.

All of a sudden we heard a noise that sounded like the
cellar door opening. We looked at each other with stares of
question. Next, scratching on the bathroom door again.
It has to be one of the cats this time. Nope! I open the
bathroom door and Bronson is sitting in the hallway again.
NO WAY!!!! Right now my mind is completely blown. I'm
speechless. I look at Kerry and she says, "What The ....!" I
close the door and leave Bronson in the hallway and tell
him not to scratch the door and lay down, which he did.
Bronson was an amazing dog. The first of four for us. All
equally amazing in their own right and very obedient.

I sat down again with Kerry. "Did you let the dog upstairs Anna?" She pointed to "NO" on the board. "Then who?" I asked.

"Alexander," she replied.

"He likes the dog?" I asked. "YES," she said. Well… That was enough for me. At this point Kerry and I felt exhausted. We decided to stop. At least we got some answers, if any were even slightly true. I told Anna, if it's possible, to come into my dreams and show me everything I need to know or what she may want me to know. I was not doing the Ouija board again. We asked Anna to blow out the candle when she left and said "Goodbye" to her on the board. Kerry and I closed the bathroom door behind us with the candle still flickering. We went downstairs to the kitchen in awe of what had just happened and completely dumbfounded. We both agreed that we needed to try and figure out what was going on here. We waited about thirty minutes and went back up to the bathroom. As we opened the door we saw the smoke from the candle wafting in the air. The candle was extinguished.

Not long afterward, one night after watching TV we kissed, said our good nights and assumed our sleeping positions. I had an eerie feeling I was being watched. I opened my eyes and there was 'HIM.' A tall, lanky slender man that was wearing a period-type suit. Black pants, black jacket, and white shirt, with a bit of a frill on the collar. He looked a bit like how you see Abraham Lincoln dressed back in the day, but this guy didn't have the beard or top hat. I was staring at him and in my head thinking, "Who the hell are you and why are you standing by my bedside?" He glared back with an angry scowl on his face. I blurted out, "WHO ARE YOU & WHAT DO YOU WANT?" He started reaching his hands down to me, but I woke up almost hyperventilating and sitting straight up. Kerry woke up and asked me what was wrong. I replied, "I just had a really bad dream."

"Of what?" she asked.

"Nothing, I'll tell you in the morning if I remember it. Let's go back to sleep." No sooner did I fall asleep then there he was again. "HIM!" Who is this guy and why is he on the side of my bed again. I asked again, "WHO ARE YOU AND WHAT DO YOU WANT!?" I then said, "You're not even real. I'm dreaming." Just then he said, "I am real and now you will know!" He reached down and forcefully grabbed both of my biceps and pulled me straight up out of bed as I flipped over and landed on the floor at the end of the bed. I awoke from my dream and I was actually on the floor at the end of the bed. Kerry woke up again and asked loudly, "What the hell are you doing?" I was completely stunned. "Kerry, I don't know what just happened!" I blurted out. My body was sore and my arms really hurt like they had been viciously tugged on. I crawled back into bed and went back to sleep, reluctantly.

In the morning when I woke up, I was really sore. Kerry

was already up and was downstairs. She's an early riser but me, not so much. I went into the bathroom to wake up, brush my teeth and do the regular morning ritual stuff when I noticed them. I had five finger bruises on both of my biceps. I completely freaked out! I totally remembered EVERYTHING about last night's dreams and "HIM." "Kerry," I yelled, "Come up here now!" I showed her the bruises and explained to her what had happened in my dreams, and apparently for real.

"Anna Marie told us about 'HIM.' I now know there is a 'HIM.' I don't know who this guy is or what he wants but we need to get him out of here NOW!"

The very next night before I went to bed I said out loud, "I need to know who you all are, why you're here, what I can maybe do to possibly help you and get you the fuck out of my house. Come to me in my dreams because they are obviously some sort of weird reality and tell me the story." I went to sleep and it started again. There he was right next to my bed again. Without him moving his lips I heard him say in my head, "I told you I was real and if you don't help me you will continue to know!"

"Help me help you or make like a tree and leave!" I said angrily back at him. Bad move on my part. He wasn't impressed and again put one hand on my forehead pushing my head hard into the pillow while his other hand was pushing down with such force on my chest. It felt like I was being crushed and my neck was going to snap. I woke up gasping for air. Kerry awoke and actually saw my head being pushed into my pillow. She frantically started calling my name and asking me what to do. I was awake but couldn't speak. She was about to dial 911 for an ambulance because she thought I was having a heart attack, stroke or some other serious medical issue. I mustered enough strength to yell, "GET OFF OF ME!!!" He let me go and stopped his attack, but this was only the beginning.

Kerry and myself in 1992

CHAPTER 7
Let The Body Hit The Floor

I t was a Saturday night. We spent most Friday and Saturday nights getting ready to go out and party it up a little. Well, sometimes it was more than a little. Time to go out rockin' for the night to see some friends and their band play at a local Chinese restaurant/dive bar. I/We spent so much time at The Kahala. I was either playing shows myself, getting drunk watching friends play, or sitting in with whatever band was playing for a song or two. The Kahala was the go-to club for a lot of us back then. Some friends from an older band I was formally in, decided to get back together. They recruited another drummer friend of mine and were playing in an Alice In Chains Tribute band called "Grind." We had a fun night hanging with friends and as the night wound down after the show, said our goodbyes and headed home. Mike asked, "Do you guys want to go over to Bickford's with us for breakfast?"

"No thanks bud, not tonight. The food in that place never sits right and may be worse than Denny's, if that's possible. I have to be really drunk to be in Bickford's mode, and I'm not even close," I chuckled back.

Kerry and I made our way home. We both ended up having bowls of cereal just to take the hunger pangs away before going up to bed. She started again, "Something doesn't feel right in here. The air feels heavy and just doesn't seem right."

"Kerry," I said, "It's nothing. There's nobody here." She came back at me quickly, "I'm telling you, something is not right and I can feel it."

"No!" I exclaimed, "It's probably the alcohol and you just need to sleep it off." She had been bringing up the past incidents constantly. While I was trying to forget about it and keep her calm about everything that was going on, she wouldn't let it go.

She really started getting upset with me because I kept shrugging off her concerns and feelings as just paranoia with a side of peppermint schnapps. As I started up the stairs to our bedroom I said to her sternly, "There's nothing here, so knock it off and let's just go to bed." I made it up three steps when all of a sudden I felt a strong grip of hands on both of my biceps again. The force actually lifted me off the steps into the air and threw me back against my front door at the bottom of the stairs. I was high enough that the back of my head hit the top of the door frame and with the force of my body hitting the door, the heel of my right foot put a four inch crack in the door panel. This door is from the sixties and solid wood. The crack is still there today. When I see the sunlight creep through the crack it's a reminder that we may still have guests in our home. Welcomed or not.

Crack in lower left door panel on a sunny day. Photo taken on 9/12/24

At that time, NOT WELCOMED!

The impact of me hitting the door knocked me out cold. Kerry came running over to me shaking me and yelling my name. I started regaining consciousness but I was really stunned. "Look up the stairs," she said. It took me a minute or so to comprehend what she was saying. "Did you see that? At the top of the stairs?"

"No! What?" I asked. " The green mist hovering at the top of the stairs," she said. By the time I turned to look it was gone. I stood up and said out loud, "Okay, I get it. You definitely exist! Please don't hurt me or us. I will do my best to help you with whatever it is that you want." I had been kind of blowing everything off until that point. When it came up in conversation with Kerry, I had to play it off and make some lame excuse about what was happening. I had even said I must have had a violent dream to cause the previous marks on my arms and somehow threw myself out of bed. I knew in my mind it really happened and I sounded extremely stupid trying to rationalize everything to Kerry. Getting thrown off the stairs, knocked unconsciousness and her seeing a green mist was no joke. There were no more excuses or ridiculous scenarios I could make up to make Kerry feel more at ease. We were both wide awake and not dreaming. This incident was unmistakably as real as a heart attack and now we needed to figure out some kind of plan.

Kerry grabbed the phone book and dialed the number to Bickford's. "What are you doing?" I asked. "I'm calling to see if Mike will come over for the night and stay with us."

"Why?" I asked. "Because!" she said.

"Umm, okay?" I replied.

Mike came over and we told him what had happened. He didn't tell us we were nuts and really listened and understood the anxiety Kerry and I had. However, he was a non-believer and made up scenarios of possibilities of what could have happened. By this point it was around three o'clock in the morning or later. We all went to sleep. In the morning, Kerry called for Mike. "Come over here in the hallway. Do you feel that?" She asked. He replied, "No, I don't feel anything."

"Okay," she said, "Sit on the top step of the landing next to me."

Mike sat down and immediately said, "Whoa, it's extremely cold right here!"

"Explain that," she said. He got up and walked a few steps, then back to where he was sitting. The air went from cold to warm and normal then back to cold. Kerry got up and moved a few feet away from the top step and the cold air followed her right to where Mike was. After a few minutes, the cold went away and it was a normal temperature again like the rest of the house. Mike still didn't agree one hundred percent that something weird or abnormal was happening, but he also didn't try to disclaim it. Instead he left with, "Are you guys okay now?" Kerry nodded and Mike said, "I'm out. Good luck and if you need me again, just call."

What are we going to do to get rid of this spirit, demon, pissed off, dead old, Abe Lincoln looking guy? It kept running through my head. Kerry and I decided to do some investigating. The more information we could find the better we'd be able to understand what was going on, and more so, why. I also needed to find solid facts, so I definitely knew this wasn't all in my head. I kept telling myself, "You're not crazy! How could you have physical marks on your body, be flipped out of bed or thrown against a door if it was just in my mind?" I really started believing it couldn't be possible. "Kerry, let's go to the library with the information you wrote down from the Ouija board chat we had with Anna and see what we can possibly dig up," I mentioned. "It's worth a shot," she agreed and said she was thinking the same thing. We headed to the library in town and asked at the desk how we could go about finding any information about the land our house was currently on and what it may have been in the past.

The librarian said, "All of the city's history and archives of Nashua are in The Hunt Room."

"Well," I asked, "What is the Hunt Room and how do we gain access to it?"

"Easy," she said, "I've got the key. You both need to get me immediately when you're done in here so I can lock it up." I kind of felt like we were in a Nancy Drew and The Hardy boys TV episode, ghost sleuthing. I was obviously the rocker-like Shaun Cassidy. We were in that room for hours combing through microfiche clips, newspaper articles, and land deed records. I found a bunch of books that ended up being registry records of what the city looked like back in the early 1800s. At some point, the land on which my house was built was mostly farmland - acres and acres of land. In the early 1800s there was a farmhouse that was owned by one of the wealthiest families in the area, The Spauldings. It looked like they had a housekeeper that was listed in the registry. Her name : Anna Maria! "Kerry," I said with excitement and a little nervous tone in my voice, "YOU'VE GOT TO SEE THIS!"

Anna Maria with no last name given worked for the family as a housekeeper and resided on the property with her young son, Alexander. Alexander's age was listed as seven or eight years old, and Anna Maria's as her late twenties. The dates and time period matched up from Kerry's notes she had taken. We were literally shaking with unsettledness, but excited we had found a few facts. Later in the early 1900s, a gentleman by the name of Marcel Theriault owned and lived on this same farm area. He died in a plane crash on June 17th, 1928 at the age of 43. He was in the books in The Hunt Room as one of New Hampshire's 100 notable people. His grave marker said, Lawyer/Farmer. How do I know this, you may be asking yourself? Well, when I was a young teenager, myself and some friends found his grave. It was one grave marker with a short stone wall around it and it was at the end of what is now Coliseum Ave in Nashua, New Hampshire, and just before the entrance heading into Lincoln Park at the end of the street. His body was moved and any sign of the original grave has been removed as apartment buildings were built in the mid 1990s. It was a well known party spot to hang out and drink and get high for the area kids that knew about it.

Kerry and I had all this new information from different time periods and we really didn't know if any of it was related to the people in my dreams or just random facts. "Let's get out of here," I said to Kerry. "We have enough to start with and we've been here most of the day."

She agreed and we left, telling the librarian to lock up the room. "What are we going to do now?" Kerry asked,

"Ask for more pieces of this wild puzzle, I guess," I responded.

That night, before we went to sleep, I said out loud, "Come into my dreams and somebody show me what I need to know to help you." Over the next four nights I kept having the same dream but every night it seemed to go a little further. It started out with a woman who I believed was Anna Maria on a farmer's porch with a young boy. I assumed this was her son, Alexander. Up strolls the pissed off Abe Lincoln looking guy, but looking younger and happier. He motions to Alexander to come with him. The boy looked excited and playful as they both left the house with a dog and moved across the land. They were heading towards the Nashua River with what looked to be some type of hand-made fishing poles. They appeared to have been crudely constructed with sticks and string. The dog was running, barking and jumping around the boy. They looked like they had a good bond. As they got to the river, which is pretty deep, the boy was tossing rocks into the water. It seemed like the older guy was maybe yelling at him to stop because he was scaring the fish away. There was no sound but the arm flailing and hand gestures seemed to indicate that the guy was aggravated at the youngster. I don't remember Alexander ever trying to fish. He was playing with the dog upstream of where the guy was trying to fish. Then I woke up! I yelled for Kerry, " I have some of the picture." I explained what I had seen from the dream but I still didn't know angry Abe's name.

There's more to his story and more I need to see. I think some more progress is being made. I have to know the whole story. I was so obsessed that I almost couldn't wait to go to sleep after a day hoping I'd get more answers. Well, I did and it wasn't what I was hoping for.

Chapter 8

Malfador, I Can't Fix This!

While I was driving at work delivering auto parts a week or so later, I kept hearing a voice in my head. It was almost as a voice was whispering in my ear. "Get the movie! Witchboard! Get the Movie! Witchboard! It will help you understand me!" Again, this is happening mid-morning while I'm driving for work and not in a dream. I called Kerry at home. Her friend and co-worker at the time, Mary, was at our house hanging out with her. I told her that I kept getting this strange feeling in my gut and voices in my head. "Kerry, you need to go rent a movie called Witchboard."

"Why?" she asked.

"I'm being told that there are some clues or situations in the movie like ours that may help us understand what's going on in our house and with the spirits that are there." Neither of us had ever heard of the movie. She agreed to go try and find it at our local Blockbuster movie rental store and would report back if she thought there was anything worth reporting. Well... she called me a couple hours later.

"Jéan, you're not even going to believe me. You just need to get home as soon as possible and watch this movie!"

I arrived home and we threw the tape back in the VCR. "Kerry, haven't you heard of or read the sticker?"

"What sticker?" she said.

"Be kind and rewind." While I waited for the tape to rewind to the beginning, she started telling me about some of the similarities between our life and what happens to a couple in this movie. They agreed to watch the movie again with me. The movie starts with a couple that goes to a party where people are messing around with a Ouija board for entertainment. Chris and I did this years ago, but by ourselves. Kerry and I had just done this recently. The couple in the movie would have arguments over small senseless issues because the female was playing with the Ouija board by herself while her boyfriend was away. Apparently she was being enticed by the spirit of a playful boy. Neither Kerry and I were using the board at home at this point, or alone, and didn't again after our session with Anna Marie. That was the time Bronson, our dog, was unleashed and came upstairs with the help of Anna Marie's playful boy Alexander. However, in the movie they call a medium over to their home for a seance and house cleansing. The medium in the movie tells the couple that spirits can manipulate the living around them and at times cause stress and turmoil. Thus causing people to argue and cause relationship issues. Kerry and I found that interesting only because since the spirit issues started for us, we had been having a lot more disagreements with each other and personal issues. We actually had a group with a medium and supposedly intuitive people over to cleanse our home. The medium said she felt there were a couple people that were close to us here, like family members. However, there were people here who were not supposed to be here and were not friendly. You don't say?! Whatever they did, didn't work. Back to the movie. All of a sudden, there on my TV set was a pretty good resemblance of the spirit of angry Abe, as I've been calling him. His name in the movie was Malfador. The definition of Malfador is "Evil One" or a wicked, sinful person.

This struck a huge chord with me. The rest of the movie didn't apply to Kerry nor I. The moral of the movie was basically don't play with a Ouija board because it can open a portal between the dead realm and the realm of the living. That was the answer to the first piece of this supernatural puzzle. Chris and I years earlier may have allowed some of these ghosts into my house. The name that showed on the board, "Evil," Angry Abe, or "Malfador," as we'll now call him, may have been given a way to come into my house or my realm to communicate all those years ago. Who else might have come through? It certainly wasn't Randy Rhoads or Led Zeppelins' John "Bonzo" Bonham. I then suspected that the young boy, Alexander, may have been in my home since I was young. He possibly could be the playmate I had when I was really young. Was Alexander "Little Boy?" I feel since he's been the only young boy spirit I'm aware of in my house that he is in fact "Little Boy."

Kerry said to me, "We need to figure this out. Mary is a non-believer in the supernatural and paranormal. Do the Ouija board again with her and see if you can get more answers. I'll write them down again if anything seems pertinent." With our legs crossed and the Ouija board on our laps, I asked, "Are you here with us right now?"

Mary & myself

The planchette moved to "Yes."

"Is this the man in the suit that looks like Malfador from the movie that's in my dreams?" Again, the planchette moved to "Yes."

"I need to know what you want me to do? I keep asking you to show me in my dreams." The planchette moved and spelled "Help or Pain." I asked out loud, "Are you saying if I don't help you you will cause more pain for me?" The answer was a definitive, "YES!"

"What are you going to do that could be worse than yanking me out of bed or throwing me off my stairs against a heavy wood door? I don't like being threatened!" I exclaimed out loud. There was a minute or so that the planchette wasn't moving. Just then the Ouija board and planchette flew straight off our laps into the air about three or four feet. It startled Mary so much that she kicked her legs apart to jump up quickly. In the process, she ended up kicking me between my legs in the family jewels. I let out a loud grunt as I fell over sideways holding my twig and berries in pain. After the pain subsided I said out loud, "Okay, I get the point and once again you've caused me pain. Show me the whole story in a dream so I can get on with my life and get you out of it."

That night as I'm sleeping, the dream starts. It began just as it had from before when Malfador, Alexander and his dog headed to the river to go fishing. It played out almost exactly as it had before, but this time there was more to it. The dream continued and it was like a panoramic view but they were all on the other side of the bank next to the river. I couldn't see them. Suddenly, Malfador comes walking up from the river and over the bank carrying Alexander in his arms. The dog is running around them and appears to be barking again but with concerned movement. The young boy's body is dripping wet and limp in Malfadors' arms. Again, there is no sound but I have to go by what I can see. It's like watching a silent movie. He carries the boy back to the house. Anna Maria comes out onto the porch. I'm guessing the dog barking incessantly got her attention. She starts running towards Malfador and Alexander with her arms outstretched. They meet in front of the farmer's porch. Anna Maria and Malfador are exchanging words and it looks like a pretty heated and intense verbal exchange. Watching this gave me a feeling in my stomach like when you feel something is terribly wrong – like an uncomfortable knot in the gut. Then really swiftly, Anna Maria slapped Malfadors' face, took Alexander in her arms and moved quickly into the house.

She laid him on a couch and as Malfador was making his way into the home, she pushed him back out the door and basically slammed it in his face. The dream ended with Malfador walking off the porch away from the house with his head hung low. Then the scenery changed. It was no longer the house and field, it was Malfador standing at the side of my bed like he had done before. This time, he had a look on his face of sadness and despair.

As I'm still dreaming I asked him, "Did Alexander die?" He nodded slowly. "Did you ever talk to Anna Maria again?" I asked. He moved his head side to side. "So you want me somehow to get you back together with Anna Maria?" He nodded "Yes" again. Going through it again feels like the dream was last night. It's still ingrained in my brain so vividly.

I remember saying to him, "Look, I am extremely sorry this happened to you, Alexander and Anna Maria. I truly am. I just don't see nor do I know how to communicate to or with her to help you. I am not a medium and really don't know how to go about this. I don't even know how I am talking to you." I stated, "Please don't hurt me or bother us in our home anymore." I told him, "You are free to stay here with her and around her and Alexander if they're here, but as far as my help getting you both together again, it's not possible. I'm not the right person to help you. I hope someday she will talk to you and accept your forgiveness." I then asked, "Will you please let Kerry, my father and I lead our lives here and not interfere anymore?" He again nodded with a "Yes."

Was it finally over? Did I make peace with a ghost? It seemed that a terrible accident had happened on Malfadors' watch and Alexander drowned in the river while playing with his dog. It also seemed Malfador just wanted to talk to Anna Maria again and receive some sort of forgiveness. I never could tell if they were married or if Alexander was both of theirs or just Anna Maria's child. Still a lot of unanswered questions, but none that I ever felt needed to be answered. I still don't even know what Malfador's real name is. Could it be Abe, or something easy like Bob? I don't know. These past three chapters covered about a ten year time span. Kerry and I were contacted by the producer of the cable network TV show "A Haunting" about our story. We told them the main stories of what happened, which I just told to you, and they wanted to use them for their series. The issue we had was that they would have actors play Kerry and I and they may embellish some of the story to make it more exciting for TV. We declined immediately, as we didn't want to be involved in something that they may show as not being true to what happened to us. We weren't looking for a quick buck or attention from this. In fact, only family or a few close friends were ever told about this ghost story for fear of potential ridicule. Everything that happened was unsettling to us and in some instances extremely bothersome.

As for Malfador, our paths crossed briefly one more time. I believe he's still here along with Alexander and I have what I feel is proof. More on this later. Anna Maria has never come back to talk to us. Maybe she can't without the help of the Ouija board, and we're not EVER going down that road again. Not in our house!

Chapter 9

I Thought You Didn't Believe In Life After Death?

On February 23rd, 1999, I went to visit my father the day before his seventy-fifth birthday. I didn't know that would be the last time I would ever see him, as he passed away a few hours after our visit. My father had been in a nursing home for a little less than a year because he started displaying signs of dementia the previous year. Driving back home one evening from visiting his brothers and sisters in Lowell, a trip he'd made thousands of times, he somehow drove northward on Route 3 to New Hampshire, but in the southbound lane. It was a foggy night, so it's plausible that he became disoriented. I arrived home after playing a local show only to find my father was home, but his car was not.

"Dad, where is your car and who brought you home?"

"I don't know!" He looked extremely confused and then slid a paper over to me on the kitchen counter. It was a warning summons from the Nashua Police Department for driving the wrong way on the highway at 11:30 pm.

"Dad - are you kidding me?!" I blurted out.

I called the Nashua Police to gather some details. They told me Dad's car had been impounded and where I could find it. I asked the officer if my father's driver's license would be revoked for this violation. I actually wanted it to happen - for his safety and for that of everyone else on the road. If I had committed the same offense, I have no doubt that I would have been arrested and thrown in the slammer. I was thankful Dad was home and safe, but sadly, I was forced to face what I had been witnessing over a period of months: the decline of my father's mental awareness.

"There's nothing I can do legally," the officer stated.

I asked him, "Will you play along with me and tell my dad his license has to be turned in to me so I can send it to the proper authorities for revocation? I will just take his license and tell him he can't drive anymore, and he'll be none the wiser."

Fortunately, the officer agreed.

We offered our little shenanigan-white-lie to my father, and after he ended his phone call with the officer, he handed his license to me. I told him I'd take care of it, and that he could no longer drive. This didn't last long.

One day shortly thereafter, I arrived home from work to find his car was in a different spot in the driveway.

"Dad," I asked, "did you take the car out for anything today? Any type of errands?"

"No, I didn't. I've been home all day," he replied.

I didn't believe him one bit, but I wouldn't have been surprised if he had forgotten that he did. The next morning, concerned my father might drive off again, I placed a piece of peanut M&M candy by his tire. Sure enough, I returned home to find the M&M squashed on the driveway pavement. My father denied taking the car, but I knew I had to come up with a way he could not drive the car, and again for the safety and well-being of others. I decided to simply disconnected the battery cable and that would be the end of it. The very next day, I came home from work and my father met me outside to greet me as I was getting out of my car.

"Jéan, my car won't start. Something is wrong!"

"Oh, really?" I replied somewhat aloofly. "I'll check it out Dad, and see if I can figure it out." Well, that didn't happen. A couple weeks went by and he started walking to the market for his daily paper, snacks, and microwavable pizzas. He also did it for exercise, which he had always done a couple of times a week anyway, even when he was able to drive.

I returned home from work one day a few weeks later to find that my father wasn't at home. The sun was setting and the sky would be dark very soon. Where was he? Just then my phone rang. It was from a switchboard operator from a business in downtown Nashua four miles away. My father was in the lobby, lost and disoriented. During his walk, he apparently had gone astray from his regular route and ended up downtown. I quickly drove to pick him up and waited no longer to have "the talk" with him – the discussion that no one wants to have with their parents. My father was not safe being alone anymore. After carefully belaboring over the various points and cautiously approaching the conversation so as to not compromise my father's dignity, he agreed.

As I was trying to figure out the next steps that Kerry and I needed to take in this transitional process, my father again went out on his own for a walk to the store. For all I knew, he may not have even remembered our chat. While I was at work, my neighbor called me and said my father had fallen near the end of our street on a patch of black ice. She had called an ambulance for him, and he was at the hospital. Immersed in feelings of intense guilt thinking that I was to blame, I rushed to the hospital. I couldn't get answers fast enough from health care services to help my dad. Was this my fault? I couldn't tie him to a chair and say, "STAY!"

After the hospital's evaluation of my father's mental state, the resetting of his dislocated shoulder from his fall, and enduring thousands of questions about our home arrangements and work schedules, I was informed that my dad wouldn't be returning home with us. In addition to this shock, we also needed to find a nursing home for him - within three days. Social workers wanted to relocate my dad to a state-run facility way up in the northern woods of

New Hampshire.

"NO WAY!" I firmly stated.

Dad's brothers and sisters, who were still alive, were all in their late sixties to eighties. If moved so far away, he'd never see them again. After a laborious fight with "the system," I was able to find a home for him at a fantastic nursing home in Lowell, Massachusetts, just down the street from his family. It looked like a southwestern villa on the outside, and a swanky high-end hotel on the inside; thankfully, it didn't smell of urine and feces like most nursing homes sadly do. However, as I mentioned earlier, my dad was in there a little less than a year.

I was going to visit him, have dinner with him, or taking him out for dinner at least three to four times a week, every week. Sometimes we'd play cards or watch TV. He had moments when he was extremely lucid and seemed perfectly fine, but then his mind would slip off to somewhere else.

Dad's sister-in-law, my Aunt Joanne, was a part of the weekend card playing crew that my dad would visit. She would go and visit him on a regular basis during the day, while I'd catch up with him after work in the early evenings. No matter what, I called him every day, whether I was going to visit or not. At one point, I had been sick and had not seen Dad for almost two weeks because I didn't want to potentially make him ill, but his birthday was approaching, and there was no way I was going to miss it.

I walked into Dad's room with birthday gifts of new clothes to find him in bed with oxygen tubes in his nose. The nurse came in and said he'd been having a hard time breathing at times, so they added oxygen to help him. We talked a little, but I did more of the talking and he did more of the nodding "yes" or shaking his head "no" in response to my questions, maintaining his side of the conversation. I could see he looked a bit sleepy. He pulled my arm towards him and gave me a kiss on the forehead. That in itself was odd. To this day, I can only remember my father saying, "I love you" to me a few times. More so, kissing me on the cheek or forehead was something he stopped doing after I was very young. I knew he loved me and showed it in other ways, just not that way.

"Jéan, I love you, but I have to quit," he said.

"You look tired, Dad. Happy birthday and I'll call you tomorrow." I told him, "I love you also." I kissed him on the forehead and made my way out.

As I was leaving, I looked back at him; he nodded and waved goodbye.

I headed home, as I was hosting rehearsal with the band in which I was playing at the time, "Flesh Tuxedo." Great band name, right? If you know, you know; if you don't, then watch the movie Spinal Tap. After rehearsal I headed upstairs to bed around 10pm, when I all of a sudden felt sick to my stomach. My body went through this wave of nausea for about ten minutes. I didn't end up physically sick, but something wasn't right. I got into bed and turned on the TV for our regular nightly ritual. Out of nowhere, my mind, my focus, and my head turned to stare at the phone. Within about five seconds it rang. Everyone knows late night calls are usually never good.

"Hello, is Jéan or Kerry there?" the voice asked.

"Yes, this is Jéan," I replied.

"I'm sorry to tell you ... that your father has passed away."

"WHEN?" I asked her.

"About ten minutes ago," she said. "I assume you'll be coming down?"

"Yes," I uttered. "I'll be there in thirty minutes."

Kerry and I grabbed our jackets and headed out.

As we were driving down it occurred to me. He had stated, "I have to quit." I didn't realize it at the time but he was telling me he was all done and had to quit living. Once we arrived, I went into the room while Kerry stayed in the lobby. I never thought he would die about five hours after seeing him, and about two hours before his seventy-fifth birthday. After some personal time and talking to him again and hoping he would hear me, I called my Aunt Joanne. Now, I was the person calling late into the night with bad news. My aunt informed me that she hadn't been down to visit my dad because she had also been sick for the past two weeks, but she had visited with him earlier that night for a short time, not long after I had left. I missed seeing her by minutes. I hung up the phone and turned to my dad, thanking him for waiting to see us both before he willed himself to leave this earth. That is some serious strength and brain power, the underestimated brain power of a person with dementia. How incredibly amazing to know that we all have that much power in our minds to control our bodies. It reminds me of patients who are allergic to anesthesia or pain medication, yet endure surgical incisions, having the mind control to not feel a knife cutting into them. Apparently, it's possible to call it a day and end your life if and when you want just by determination and mind control.

So, if you recall, my father refused to believe in the paranormal, life after death, ghosts, or spirit entities. The last words I said to my father before they closed his casket at the funeral home was "Dad, I know you don't believe in ghosts or messages after you die, but I believe one hundred percent that it's possible. Please, please, please if you're able, come back to me in my dreams, in human form - or however possible - and give me some sign that you are alright. Show me that you are with your brothers and sisters who passed before you. Show me something, anything."

One night, the week after he had passed, in the middle of the night, I sat up in bed and stared into the darkness of my bedroom toward a window that had a little moonlight streaming through.

"Dad, is that you?" I said in my head.

I was staring at a silhouette of my father's profile.

No words were spoken aloud, but I heard his voice speaking in my head.

"Jéan, I am okay, and I'm with my brothers and sisters and my parents. I heard you talking to me at the nursing home and your phone call to Joanne. I also heard you at the funeral home, and here I am to let you know that I'll be alright - and you will be also. We will see each other again someday when it's meant to be. I believe you now, and I'm sorry I didn't in the past. I have to go now, but I'll check in when I can, and I'll always be around. Do well."

That was it. Then the shadow disappeared. I remembered feeling a warm calm wash over me, and the stress of him being in a nursing home, being ill, and now being gone subside. Was this just a dream? Am I dreaming all of this? I physically pinched my arm and felt it. I was still sitting up in bed and looked over at Kerry, still asleep next to me. I could hear her breathing. I was totally awake. I just laid my head back on my pillow, feeling happy that my Dad was okay and he'd be around when he could.

That Friday of the same week I was running late from work to get home, shower and load up my drums to head out for a gig. That was all I had on my mind, and I was intensely focused upon arriving at the venue as soon as possible; I knew I'd receive an earful from my band-mates if I was late. As I entered the house, I stopped dead in my tracks. I was in the kitchen, passing the hallway into the dining room to head upstairs to shower, and there he was. I saw my father come out of the downstairs bathroom and go into the living room on the other side of the staircase, the room once considered the scary room that no one liked. Kerry and I had turned that into our regular living room with our TV, so we were in there daily. I ran down the hallway into the room where I saw my dad go but he wasn't there. I saw him! No doubt in my mind. The oddest part was that he didn't have any legs. His head was at the same height as he would have been in life, but he had no legs. He was just a torso in his favorite black and red plaid button down shirt. I could see through him to the den door behind him. He never looked in my direction, facing straight ahead as he moved into the living room.

Those were the only times I remember seeing him, but on a few occasions, I have heard his voice calling my name when I'm alone in the house. He's one of the only people who actually pronounces my name correctly in the French dialect. That's how I know it's him.

I hope my father is still one of the spirits in our house, but I haven't seen or heard from him in years, so he might have completely passed to the other side by now. I'd like to believe he's still around, and now I know he's aware of something more, an existence after we die. My father finally validated me and my story of seeing his brother, Arthur. Now they are together, along with his other fifteen siblings.

My father and I. Maybe he was unconsciously getting me used to having long hair and being a musician at a young age. I always found this photo funny & somewhat prophetic.

Chapter 10

I Don't Understand Why

As I mentioned in the forward, at times I have premonitions of people who have passed trying to contact me. It runs the gambit of how it happens, from ...... to ......, and my guess is as good as yours as to why it happens. Years ago, I had a good friend, Chris, with whom I was in a band back in 1987 and 1988. We were acquaintances prior to playing together in the band, but after playing together, and right up until his passing in May of 2005, I considered us very good friends. Back when we played together, we were in our early twenties, and we partied - a lot. There would be times after drinking way too much and throwing darts that I'd end up sleeping on Chris's couch.

One morning, Tammy, Chris's wife, looked at me and said, "Jéan, What is it? You look like you're in deep thought!"

I don't think at that time I gave her a straight answer, as I really wasn't sure myself what I was contemplating. I remember that was around the time I started having premonitory dreams more often, and at times I could hear whispering in my ears. I began to notice, much like when I saw the train derailment and crash not long before, I was able to drift off deeply enough to snag some sleep. This was because I had either been extremely exhausted, or I'd been drinking, and my mind was more relaxed.

Eventually, I confided in Tammy, and told her what was happening to me. Sometimes, when I was around a group of people - close friends or family - I would experience images, almost like silent movies, or I'd see situations that included either Tammy or Chris in them. These visions were not unlike the Malfador incident, but they were much more brief and to the point.

Chris was an excellent self-taught drummer, and he also played guitar, as I do. During our time as band-mates, he played drums and I was one of the guitarists. We had a very unique musical bond. The day before he unexpectedly passed, we had chatted about a show he had to play the next night, on Friday, but he was free that Saturday, and he had planned to come see my band play at a club at the beach. I was looking forward to it, as I couldn't attend his show on Friday because I was also playing a gig.

On that Saturday morning, I received a text from a friend who said someone in Chris's band had passed away outside the venue where they were playing, but he didn't know who it was. I called one of the other band members, only to sadly learn that it was Chris who had died. To say I was shocked and unbelievably sad would be an understatement. At that time in my life, I was thirty-eight years old and I hadn't lost many close friends. Chris was only two years older than me, and he passed much too soon.

After receiving such horrible news, I still had to drive up to Hampton Beach, New Hampshire to perform. I kept talking out loud in my truck to him.

"Chris, what the hell happened? What took you from all of us? We were supposed to hang out tonight! I'm so sad and pissed off because you're gone - you're not supposed to be!"

"Chris, if it's possible, please come to me and tell me what happened. Show me what happened!"

Myself and Chris in 1987 while playing in the same band. A dark artsy type of photo.

That gig was a hard one for me, and I played my drums like never before. I left every ounce of energy, angst, sadness, and fury on that stage! If my drums and cymbals could talk, they would have been screaming in pain as I hit them.

By the time I arrived home, I was completely exhausted, more so than most shows I've played. I climbed into bed and fell fast asleep.

And there he was in my dream; Chris came to me. He told me to pass along an extremely descriptive message to Tammy. I won't share what the message was because it was private and between Chris and Tammy, but the gist of it relates to how he saw her and heard what she was saying while she was making her way to the hospital, and when she received the devastating news. Chris showed me short snippets of how his show went down the night before and some of the outcome. The rest was filled in by his band-mate on the morning I spoke to him.

Upon waking, I immediately called Tammy to tell her about my dream. I wasn't sure if it was completely just a dream, but it felt so different than a regular, ordinary dream ... even though I usually don't remember ordinary, random dreams. During the phone call to Tammy, I remember having a hard time getting it all out because I knew deep down that if it was all true, it would be a bit traumatizing for her. I don't like upsetting anyone, but because this message was so descriptive, I knew it would hit hard.

"Jéan, spill it!" she commanded sternly. "Tell me everything!"

I laid it all out because it was so vivid, like Chris was on the left side of a picture-in-picture TV, and what he was showing me was on the right side. At times, he would pause the picture and tell me things. Almost as if he would freeze the frame and say, "I heard what she was saying here." Then he told me what it was. Then resume the playback of the next scene. When I finished telling Tammy everything I knew about that night and gave the message to her from Chris, there was a long pause on the other end of the phone.

"There's NO WAY you could have known some of what you just told me, Jéan! I was alone in my car, talking out loud, driving to the hospital. How do you know what I said, Jéan … HOW?!"

"Tammy, I don't know, but this is the message Chris wanted me to tell you, so I am."

A couple of weeks went by and Chris came to me one more time. I hadn't been thinking about him that day to make me have a dream that included him. He said, "Jéan, you've gotta see this! This is funny!" He did the picture in picture view again. On the left side he was laughing and on the right side was Tammy walking up some stairs wearing a long red nighttime-type shirt with yellow looking shoes and carrying something in front of her that I couldn't make out. As she went up the stairs she tripped a little. Chris found this funny enough to show me and added, "Tell Tammy to be careful going up the stairs."

I called her the next day and just asked simply, "Have you tripped on any stairs recently?"

"No," she replied, "and why are you asking me this?"

"Just let me know if you do, and then I'll tell you."

"Like, if I trip on the outside steps going into the house?"

"Yes, any steps, anywhere."

"Okay," she affirmed suspiciously, "I'll let ya know."

A couple of days went by and my phone rang. "Jéan, I just tripped coming up the stairs!"

"Okay STOP!" I said. "Let me tell you what happened. You were carrying something in front of you while going up a long set of steps. As you were walking up, you tripped and fell forward. You were wearing a long red shirt and yellow-ish shoes."

"Oh, my head!" she said.

"You hit your head? Are you okay?" I asked. "No, I didn't hit my head!" she exclaimed. "I'm trying to figure out how you know what happened and described it per-fectly. I was carrying a laundry basket up the cellar stairs while wearing Chris's red shirt, which is really long on me and his gold P-shoes." For those whom might not know,

"P-shoes" is a common term for slippers used by people of French descent. "The slippers are too big on my feet and caught the step and I tripped."

"Tammy," I said, "Chris came to me in a dream again and showed me that this would happen. He was chuckling because he thought it was funny, but he also told me to tell you to please be careful on the stairs." Chris was, and I believe is still, watching over her, their children, and now his grandchildren whenever he's able.

I believe that after people die, they will retain their same personality as when they were of the living. Good spirits will do good or maybe cause situations of divine intervention when needed, and bad spirits of evil people will cause ghostly harm or be poltergeist-type entities.

Chris and Tammy were together from very early in their teens, and I sincerely believe his love for her carried over to the other side.

At times, and mostly again when I'm extremely over-tired or settling into bed and winding down, I'll hear whispers or talking in my ears. Sometimes I can make out the words, and other times it sounds like distant chattering, almost like if you were at a party and thirty people were talking and you're trying to make out a specific conversation going on across the room. Sometime you can catch a few words and try to piece it together. That's what the whispering sounds like to me.

I awoke one night in an almost pitch-black room to see

my wife's grandmother standing at the foot of the bed on Kerry's side. "Nan," as we called her, was looking directly at Kerry while she slept, and she had her hand on Kerry's leg. When I sat up after just seeing this and opened my eyes fully, Nan disappeared. I only saw her for about five seconds or less. Kerry and her grandmother had a very close bond. She told me stories about Nan, and I did witness some interesting events first-hand for a few years while she was still alive. Nan believed in the paranormal, and from what I'm told, she actively pursued tools that are used in communication with the deceased. She passed down tarot cards and an extremely old Ouija board to Kerry. I believe her Ouija board is the one we used in the bathroom that started the whole Anna Maria situation years earlier. (It has not made an appearance out of the box since.)

After seeing Nan, I chose not to tell Kerry, at least not yet. A few days later, I awoke to the exact same scene: Nan at the foot of the bed on Kerry's side with her hand on Kerry's leg. She was looking at Kerry while she was asleep, and she never looked my way. After this, I still decided not to say anything. Maybe it was a replay of a previous dream? I was pretty sure I was awake.

One afternoon I entered our house and unexpectedly saw Nan pass across the downstairs hallway. It was almost like she had come from out of one wall and then passed through the wall on the other side of the hallway. She was just a profile as she moved along, never stopping or noticing I was standing there. She was wearing a yellow sweat-shirt and matching sweatpants. When Kerry came home from work that night, I told her about all three "Nan" sightings. I think she was a bit skeptical. Nevertheless, that night before I went to sleep, I said in my head, "Nan, please come to me and tell me something I would not know that I can relay to Kerry so she knows I'm telling her the truth and that you're watching over her."

The next morning when I woke up, I blurted out the word "Josephine" to Kerry. It was the first thought that popped into my head when I woke up.

"Jean, that's my grandmother's first name," Kerry said. Now, if I knew that I certainly didn't remember it, nor did I ever hear any of Kerry's family address her grandmother as Josephine. Everyone called her Nan, and Kerry's father and his siblings called her "Ma." Kerry was not a hundred percent convinced.

"Ask her what her middle name is," she said to me. That night, again, before I fell asleep, I asked my question aloud.

"Nan, please come to me tonight and tell me your mid-dle name. Thank you." I actually purposefully remember asking out loud so I could be certain that Kerry could hear me.

In the morning, I got out of bed to do my morning rou-tine, turning on the TV to check out the morning news and happenings. Initially, not being not fully awake, I didn't remember my question to Nan, but after about ten minutes, my brain began to wake up, and thoughts started popping into my head. I remember hearing a female voice either before I completely fell asleep or in a dream. I kept hearing a word that started with a hard "L" sound and ended in a definite "A." The middle of the word was a bit mumbled and muffled, but it had a distinct tone. "Kerry!!" I shouted loudly. "Nan's middle name sounds like Linda, but it's not Linda!" I tried sounding it out, slurring the middle of the name to play with sounds that might help me to recall.

Finally, I was so close that Kerry revealed, "Her middle name is Lydia!"

"There's absolutely no way I could have known that!" I DIDN'T know that. I never ever knew what her middle name was. I was actually a bit blown away myself.

Thoughts and premonitions like that come to me now and then. It's feels very odd to me. I've considered reading books and possibly learning more about this and how to use or control it, but honestly, I'm not sure I want to. I feel like I'll leave it to the "experts" that have already figured out to do that or the charlatans that spread their snake oil. I do think there are a lot more fakes out there preying on grief and heartstrings that search for answers to whatever despair they're going through, or joy they need to hear to start healing. I'll just take it if it comes, and if not, my head won't be so cluttered. Ultimately, I believe I'm okay with that.

Chapter II

Mom, Is That You?

My mother and I had a great and close relationship when I was young and during the last year and half of her life. She was a short Italian woman with a great sense of humor, wit, and could be extremely sarcastic. I'd even add that she found enjoyment at times from being an instigator that liked to stir the proverbial shit pot that would cause some kind of drama. My mother was diagnosed in my late adolescent years with a very rare disease that destroys the lymphatic system and caused her extreme pain and issues a lot of times when she walked, and even when she didn't. She used to spend three weeks in the hospital and then three weeks out for many years. It probably went on for her like that for over ten years or so. When I was young we were pretty tight. Once she got the disease and over time taking all the drugs she did, she changed a lot. I mean, who wouldn't. She would get depressed, angry, lash out and guess who got the brunt of it during the day after school. My father got it at night when he got home from work. I would hear them argue constantly in my early teenage years.

Not long after my sixteenth birthday in 1983, my mother and I had a huge argument. She ended up getting so mad at me while she was doped up on painkillers and kept hitting me in the legs with her metal crutches while trying to push me down the second floor staircase. She was like a zombie with no emotion in her eyes but anger. I shook her and slapped her arm and asked, "Mom, what are you doing? What is wrong with you?" She answered, "You just hit me and I'm leaving and not coming back! Tell your father I'm done with him and you!" For years I believed "I" was the cause of my parents divorce and I also held a huge grudge toward my mother for using me as her scapegoat to get out of her marriage. I'd learn later from my father that the doctors had given my mother about four years left to live. She decided if she was going to die young she was going to do everything she wanted with no ties to anyone. This included my father and I. Surprisingly, she outlived my father and went on for another thirty-three years after she left us and passed in 2016.

Over that thirty-three year span, my mom and I had a lot of rocky times but eventually both apologized to each other and worked it out for the most part. In the fall of 2014, my mother called to tell me she had lung cancer. She swore to me, "Jéan, don't worry. I've beat everything else and only the good die young." She used to tell me this all the time. So like most people that fight cancer, she went through the treatments that the doctors encouraged for months. She called me and said, "I rang the bell today! My PET scan showed no cancer so I'm good to go."

"That's great to hear mom. Congrats," I said to her. That ended up being very short-lived. The cancer came back in her lungs and brain with a vengeance. We spent some good quality time together leading up to her end.

My mom wanted a party/get-together to enable anyone that wanted to see her for the last time to do so while she was still mobile and of "mostly" sound mind. Her comment was, "Don't have a wake or celebration after I'm gone, I WANT TO BE THERE!" She wanted to invite a few of her friends from her past as well as family on both sides of my family and childhood friends she felt like a second mom to as well. She also wanted to see the touring Journey Tribute Experience band : SCARAB that I was going out on the road with and meet the guys and their wives. Kerry and I, with the help of some very close friends, put together the after-party and concert for her on Valentine's day. It just so happened that ended up being the best day for everyone. There was a lot of love in that room for my mom. It went off great and she was so happy to see everyone.

*My mother, Kerry and myself
from the Valentine's day party on
2/14/16*

The week before she unknowingly would end up going into a hospice facility, we had a pretty great conversation outside her apartment on a beautiful sunny day. I was going to be leaving in a few weeks to head out on a tour with the band SCARAB and she asked where we were going. "Well Mom, we're heading down the east coast through the Carolinas, Georgia, Alabama, Florida, Louisiana, Mississippi and Texas. Then we head up to Colorado and play our way back through Texas, Louisiana and back up the east coast states until we finish in Maine."

"I always wanted to go and see some of those states," she

said. "Tell you what, I'm coming on tour with you!"

"Mom, how will you do that, you're not healthy nor strong enough."

"You'll see," she said to me. Then I proceeded to tell her that Kerry and I had a vacation trip planned to Florida in September after the tour. "I'll be there, too, with you guys," she said. I just looked at her and smiled as if to say, sure whatever you want to do mom.

The following week, I got a call from my mom's visiting nurse saying she had called an ambulance to transport my mother to the hospice facility. Kerry and I slept up there in her room with her for the remainder of my mom's life. We had our dog DIO up there with us for a couple days also. My mom really liked DIO and he was really sweet and gentle with her. Unfortunately, one of the nurses was scared of him because he was a very intimidating looking dog with a huge Pitbull head, but his personality was the opposite of his looks, unless he was protecting Kerry and I or felt threatened. Not much threatened DIO. Sadly we had to bring DIO back home so he said his goodbyes to her. My mom went unconscious for a couple days and then she opened her eyes. She turned her head towards me and said, "We had some fun, didn't we?"

"Yes, we did, mom," I replied to her. "I love you, mom." She whispered back, "I love you, too." Those were the very last words we spoke to each other. She fell back in an unconscious state again and passed away two days later on the day after Mother's Day.

My mom loved the beach and used to say she wanted to come back as a seagull and crap on everyone that ever gave her crap in her life. "Payback is a bitch," she'd say.

One day, not long after she passed, my wife found a starling bird that seemed ill. Starlings are not birds native to our area in the Northeastern United States. How did this bird get here? Ya I know, it flew! Kerry nursed the bird back to what seemed to be good health and was planning on releasing it back to the wild. She kept saying, "Something is odd about this bird. I feel like it's a sign from your mom for something, or it is your mom's spirit."

"Stop it!" I exclaimed, "That's silly!" Not long after that the bird got out of the enclosure Kerry had it in and it flew over to my shoulder in the kitchen. It was just staring at me with it's beady little eyes. Was it going to peck at my face? It didn't do anything but stare at me. I jokingly said, "Hi mom. Is that you?" Kerry came over and took the bird onto her finger and put it back in the birdcage we had. The following day when I came home from work the bird had died and was laying at the bottom of the cage, lifeless. Was it some kind of sign from my mom, and once I acknowledged it, she left again?

I proceeded to head out on the road with the guys in the band for our tour. Every night after my drum solo, I would cross my sticks high in the air, look up and say, that one was for you mom and I love and miss you. Our tour was going along decently. We had good shows, good audiences and it was a well needed way to get my emotions out through playing my drums after what I had gone through the last few weeks with losing my mom. We played a show in Baton Rouge, Louisiana at a casino. After my drum solo, as I put my crossed drumsticks in the air, over my left shoulder about five feet away from me I see what looked like gold glitter shimmering in the air. I quickly looked to my left but it was gone as fast as it happened. There was nothing around that could have done that, but it was unmistakable. Just before we kicked into the next song after my solo I said in my head, "Mom, was that you?" The following night we were playing in Jackson, Mississippi. I proceeded to do my drum solo and again out of the corner of my eye to my left I see the gold sparkles of what looks like pixie fairy dust or glitter raining down again for a couple of seconds. Okay, so my eyes aren't playing tricks on me. It happened again, and also the next night in Abilene, Texas. These were the specific three states my mother mentioned to me that she always wanted visit. It didn't happen again the rest of the tour.

After the tour had wrapped up, I was looking forward to some much needed fun, rest and a quality hang in Florida & Disney with Kerry for a few days. I remember some odd little things happening in our hotel room. Nothing crazy just little things that make you go hmmm. Things moved and out of place or random odd feelings. One day Kerry and I decided to hang with my bandmate Brett and his wife Hope at Typhoon Lagoon and chill at the water park for the day. We had a great time on the slides and lazy river but it was time for a lunch break. The four of us grabbed our trays of food and headed over to a picnic table. We were chatting when all of a sudden we were being eyed by a nearby starling. Sure, it was eying our food but that was the second time in a few months that I had ever seen a starling in person in my lifetime. It hung around and then grabbed a French fry off the table that we put there. It then flew up onto a wood beam of the roof over where we were. The bird was staring at us while eating the fry. Kerry says, "Maybe it's your mom again giving you a sign she's around us on our trip?" I kind of wrote that off to coincidence but then changed my mind after dinner.

Brett and Hope took us over to a great Italian restaurant for dinner in downtown Celebration which is like fifteen minutes from Orlando. It was unbeknown to me that it was their idea of a do-over 50th birthday dinner that didn't go quite as planned when Kerry and I were in Florida the year before. It was a really nice gesture from them both. When we finished dinner before the dessert came, I excused myself to use the restroom. While I was in there doing what I needed, I said out loud as there was nobody else in there but me, "Mom, is that you doing things to give us signs you're with us on this trip? Is it you? Please give me a definitive sign that I can't miss or question," I asked of her. As I went over to the sink to wash my hands, I looked up at my reflection in the mirror and was taken aback. My mom's facial image overlapped my own reflection. I resemble my mom more than my father, and it was her image in the mirror also. She looked like she did when she was healthy, before getting cancer. I jumped back, startled. As soon as I saw her, she was gone. I said out loud again, "I saw you mom! I SAW YOU! Thank you for that and watching over us and being a part of our trip. Hope you're having fun, too." I went back to the table. Brett and Hope had ordered a tiramisu cake. I hate tiramisu but it was my mom's favorite dessert. She used to joke with me about eating it but I can't and really hate it. I figured it was another sign, letting me know in her sarcastic way, I'm having my cake and eating it, too. I ended up with chocolate cake. That worked for me.

The last time I saw my mom was similar to the mirror in the bathroom in the restaurant. I was at home stepping out of the shower and instead of seeing my reflection in the bathroom mirror once the moisture on the mirror cleared, I saw only my mom. My reflection was not in there or over-lapped like the restroom mirror was. It was very quick and then gone. As I type this, she is in her lighthouse urn six feet away from me. I know she's still around me and Kerry, watching over us when she can. I also believe she still moves or does stuff knowing it aggravates me and she's chuckling at her spirit hijinks from the other side. If you have a loved one that's passed, a parent, a sibling, grandparent or friend, I urge you to still talk to them like they are with you. I do this a lot when I'm alone driving. Just spill your emotions out. It's very therapeutic, plus you never know if they can hear you or not and if it's therapeutic for them also. I have to believe that the loss and separation is just as hard for those that have passed. I always say time will never heal all wounds, it just makes the wounds easier to deal with. If you still try to communicate after your loved ones have passed, I truly believe that the scar you will keep with you from the loss will be a lot smaller and not as horrifying to deal with daily.

CHAPTER 12

More Connections Through Music And Strangeness

I was playing a show in Dracut, MA at a now defunct bar called The Mammoth Road Club with the band BOTTOMS UP, in 2005. BOTTOMS UP at that time, was more of a cover band playing a wide variety of songs from The Doobie Brothers and ZZ Top to Metallica and Pantera. Since then, we became more of an original act and had the great fortune to open as a support act for many iconic rock artists like Judas Priest, Jethro Tull, Peter Frampton, Scorpions, Three Doors Down, Collective Soul and many more throughout our twenty year career. Through my forty plus years of playing live, entertaining music lovers and fans, I've had the pleasure of meeting people I never may have if I was working in a factory or selling cell phone cases at a kiosk in the local mall.

Let's get back to The Mammoth Road Club. We had just finished our first set when a loud drunk woman came up to me at the front of the stage as I was climbing out from behind my drums. "Heyyy!!! You guys know any Zeppelin or blues standards?" she asked in a gravelly voice.

I replied, "We know some Zeppelin songs but our bass player might not. He's only really been in original bands and doesn't know all the cover music the guitarist and I do, but I'll ask." She replied in her Massachusetts accent, "Ok cuz my sister wants to sing with you'se guys. She's a singer and our brother is a locally well known guitarist. We come from a musically talented family."

"Oh yeah?" I exclaimed, "Is that right?" Well, I did know the guitarist, but didn't know these two intoxicated females were his sisters.

"Hi! I'm Michele but they call me Mickey!"

"Hi. I'm Jéan but they call me Boomer!"

Michele "Mickey" & myself

"You guys know 'Rock N' Roll" from Zeppelin? I'll sing it!"

"Oh you will, will you?" I said. "Can you really sing?" I asked. Abrasively she lashed out at me. "Yeah I can sing, mother F'er!"

"Okay, fine! Let's do it!" I ripped into the drum intro for the song and off we went. Michele came in with the lyrics like a wrecking ball of power. The whole club could have heard her without a microphone in her hand. Her voice was powerful and soulful. She had a raspy tone to her voice like Janis Joplin, but in my opinion was much better and more pleasing on the ears. We finished the song, exchanged quick pleasantries on the stage and continued with our second set. After the second set was over, I went up to Mickey and said, "Great job! Very powerful voice you have."

"You should hear me when I haven't been drinking," she said with a laugh. From that day going forward, Kerry and I became friends with Mickey. Our friendship was extremely tight and close.

Fast forward to February 6th, 2022. I was playing drums in another local group called WILDSIDE. The band is a musical tribute to the hard rock and heavy metal songs of the eighties. Well, Mickey shows up and we invite her up to sing with us. She had sang this particular song many times with us in BOTTOMS UP, but this was the only time I performed with her while in WILDSIDE. The song was a favorite of ours; "Rainbow In The Dark" from one of the greatest heavy metal singers of all time, Ronnie James Dio. While we played the song, Mickey kept forgetting the words which was completely unusual for her. She knew this song backwards, forwards and sideways. Sadly, that August she got a diagnosis of tumors on her brain. That's why she started having memory issues. She didn't know why at the time but it all started to make sense. Unfortunately her health declined and she got to a place where she knew with all her treatments she wasn't going to be the same or beat the situation. We hugged and slow danced in her living room while both singing a part of "Rainbow In The Dark." She said to me, "Jéan, I'm so scared!" I replied with, "The unknown is always scary and I'm scared and scared for you also." I told her that whenever I perform that song going forward it will be for her - My dedication to her. "You'll always be my Rainbow In The Dark Mickey!"

She said, "I love that and I love you!"

Kerry and I went to visit her in the hospital in her final days in November and I asked her, "Please if you can, come back and give me a sign that you're okay and no longer in pain when you leave us all." She nodded she would and softly in a whisper said again, "I love you." I replied with, "I love you too," and kissed her forehead. Not long after, she passed.

A couple of days later she gave me a sign. I got in my

truck and turned the key in the ignition. Right away, I heard Robert Plant belting out, "It's been a long time since I've rock and rolled!" I immediately was taken back to the Mammoth Road Club gig when I met Mickey and memories of that night. In my head and out loud I said, "Mickey… I miss you along with so many. It's not fair that you're gone. You left us all much too soon." I must have been concentrating on my memories because all of a sudden was John Bonham's thunderous drum break of triplets at the end of the song. I always listen to that part being a drummer and all, but my jaw dropped when the next song started playing. It was "Rainbow In The Dark!" Are you kidding me right now?! There's absolutely no way that it could be a coincidence. Not in my mind. No Way! Mickey sent me the sign we had discussed, and after I got past the initial shock of these songs being played back to back, I smiled. She gave me the two songs I've always associated with her. The very first song we ever performed together and the very last. "Our Song!" I know she still watches over us, her family and friends. I haven't heard anything else from her but I'm taking it that no news is good news. Hopefully, she's at peace with her mom and happy.

There have been other brief strange occurrences that have happened over the years here in our house. Kerry and I had another couple over for lunch and some game fun for the afternoon at the kitchen table. We used to talk about paranormal stuff but my friend Vinny was not into it at all. I kind of felt that he may believe in the paranormal, but he didn't want any of it around him. Even more so, for anything paranormal to happen to him. We were all discussing things about it and unexpectedly we all turned to the kitchen counter because of a loud bang. We couldn't believe our eyes. There were large bottles of olive oil and balsamic vinegar on the counter that had fallen forward in unison and slid to the edge of the counter but didn't fall off. It was unmistakable and remarkable. Just then Vinny said, "Look at the time, we've gotta go!" So being pretty freaked out they left.

In 2010, I was playing drums in a KISS non-makeup tribute band called KISS'D OFF. We dressed the part of the KISS 1992 Revenge-era line-up. We had a rehearsal one evening in my basement studio and afterward, everyone left, as usual. Myself and nobody else had been down in the rehearsal area until the next rehearsal. The following week everybody came over and headed down to the basement to get to work on whatever new songs were to be added to the set list. Scott said to me, "Hey, has anyone been down here?"

"No!" I replied.

"Well then who was standing on my guitar amplifier cabinet?"

"What are you talking about?" I said.

"Look! Whose little footprints are these?"

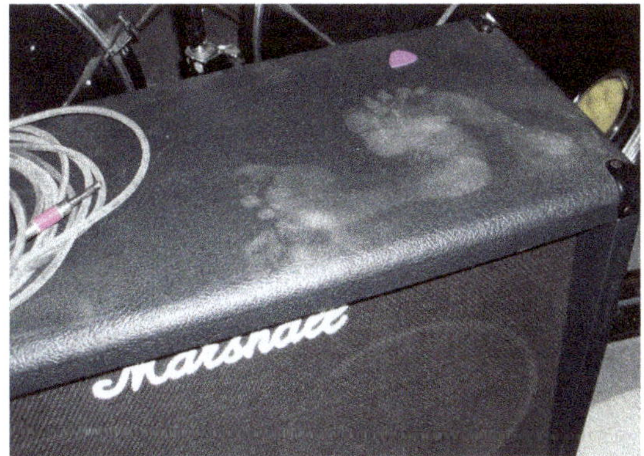

Tiny foot prints on Scott's Marshall 2x12 amplifier cabinet from dust from the basement floor

We all looked at each other completely confused. If someone was to have stood on the corner of the cabinet where the footprints are with two feet, or even one foot, the cabinet would have flipped up off the casters and been moved. It wasn't! The basement floor gets dusty and someone had to have been walking barefoot in the basement to create those footprints. It was only myself and Kerry here and those prints are smaller than our feet. Was it "Alexander?" Was it "Little Boy?"

One night, Kerry and I were sitting in the living room watching TV with the dog and cats hanging around the couch with us. We have a large decorative mirror on the wall above the couch. We heard this sizzle, static-type sound. A blue streak came between us, and a massive blinding flash of light illuminated the middle of the room. I mean it was blinding like a cars high beams straight in the eyes. It was sudden and quite shocking. It's never happened again but the theory is that mirrors are a portal between our realm and those that have crossed over and their realm. I never thought much of it until that experience but maybe there is some truth to it.

Everyone has their daily routines they do and an order in which they are done in. Where you hang your coat, leave your car keys, etc. Well, I always used to leave my wallet on the kitchen counter near my car keys so I'd have both on the way out of the door when leaving the house. One morning, I was on my way out when I couldn't find my wallet. It wasn't where I normally leave it. I checked the pocket of my leather jacket that I wore the night before, my pants pockets and everywhere near the area in case it was knocked off the counter by accident. Nothing! Nowhere to be found. Well it must have fallen out in the car the night before. Where else could it be? I tore my 1978 Bandit Edition Trans Am apart looking for it and found nothing but a couple french fries and some loose change under the seat. They get away while you're driving, too. Don't pretend it doesn't happen. You know it to be true.

I started to get stressed out a little because there was a

couple hundred dollars in there, credit cards and personal info. WHERE DID MY WALLET GO!!?? As I started to worry, I also started getting annoyed, as I needed to leave or I'd be late. I decided to go down to the parking lot at the mall where I was the night before to see if it maybe fell out of my pocket. I got in my car and drove down there but found nothing. At this point I really freaked out and got angry. I came back home and looked around the house again, both upstairs and around the downstairs rooms. Nothing! Kerry then mentioned, "Why don't you ask the spirits in our house for help, maybe they're messing with you."

"Kerry, I don't have time for anyone to be messing with me right now. I'm going to be late!"

I asked out loud in a stern voice, "If you moved my wallet or know where it is, please give it back… NOW!" I then came around the corner of the dining room and put my hand on the wooden banister as I was going to go upstairs again to check. I put my hand right on my wallet. It was on the banister at the bottom of the stairs against the bottom post. Now here's the strange part, I went up and down those stairs putting my hand in that exact spot a few times. My wallet was not there prior to me asking out loud to give it back. Strange, very strange.

I guess spirits are all around us. If you need to find something or just need help in general… ask! Every time my grandmother would lose something, I remember her telling me she would say a prayer to Saint Anthony and he would be the one that would lead her to her lost item. I don't know if Saint Anthony, my father, Nan, Malfador or invisible boy was the one to help me find my wallet. However, maybe it's possible you will get a direct answer or a sign of what you may need from a loved one, a friend or even a stranger that has passed. Apparently, they see things better than we do between both realms, may be playing jokes on us, and can be helpful too. I guess if you have a great sense of humor while alive, why couldn't you when you're dead? I will say, once I'm gone if it's possible to mess with the living, I'm on that team, as I can be a prankster. I'll wait though, no rush.

Chapter 13

My Close Friends Have Left...But Have They?

In the past six years I've had a total of fifteen close friends and a few others that were friendly acquaintances pass on. I've never felt this much loss and, at times, emptiness before in my life. I know that as time goes on and age progresses it will continue to happen and probably more frequently. I am blessed to know many people but at times it is a curse that is destined to cause sadness when they leave this earth as we know it.

The first major blow was my close childhood friend Steve in 2017. Steve was also the best man at my wedding and we stayed friends up until his untimely passing. As we got older we didn't see each other or chat as much but we always found time to connect here and there with quick texts, meetings or holidays. As life goes, paths change and growing families take up time that used to be free. When I got the news of Steve's sudden heart attack and hospitalization I was on tour with SCARAB in Louisiana. The band had just played the last show of that leg of the tour. We were on our way back to the meeting place in

Boston where we'd unload the gear and go our separate ways for awhile until the next run of shows. Another childhood friend from my neighborhood, Mike, was the one who called me. There were seven of us that were from the neighborhood and we were pretty inseparable - as tight as friends could be growing up. "Jéan," Mike said as I answered the phone, "Steve had a massive heart attack while at the city dump helping a neighbor with a tree that had fallen. He's in the hospital and unresponsive. You need to go there and I'll be there soon, too."

"I'm in Louisiana," I replied, "but I'll get there as soon as possible." Thankfully there were four of us driving back. We would usually stop around Tennessee to cut the trip in half and finish the drive the following morning. The guys knew I needed to get back to see Steve and they were all in to make that happen. We all took shifts driving straight through – something I still appreciate to this day.

Steve & I on my wedding day morning in 1994

I arrived at the hospital after a twenty-two hour drive, no shower and looking pretty tired and rough but not anywhere as rough as Steve looked in that hospital bed – hooked up with wires and tubes coming out of and off him in every direction. My eyes started to well up immediately. I talked to him for about forty-five minutes or so with no response from him. I told him he needed to pull through for his wife and daughters. This was not how he or anybody expected the way for his road of life to go. It was truly heartbreaking. I told him I'd be back, which I did a few more times, to be with him, his family and our close friends.

I got a call from his brother saying he was going to be taken off life support so I needed to go up to the hospital to say my goodbyes. He was one of the best and closest friends in my life. I returned to the hospital and chatted to Steve, reliving highlights of our youth and past. There was a time that Steve had wanted to learn how to play guitar. More acoustic guitar playing and strumming songs for fun and not expecting to tear up the guitar neck and shred like Eddie Van Halen. We both liked Guns N' Roses and Steve wanted to learn how to play the song "Patience" on guitar, so I taught him. That song and a couple songs from the Allman Brothers which Steve became a big fan of and I always related to him. I asked him at our last chat to give me a sign, if possible, that he heard me and hopefully would be doing okay on the other side wherever he would be. Deep down in my heart and gut, I knew Steve was furious that he couldn't communicate with his family and friends. Even though he couldn't talk to me, I felt the energy of him being so pissed off that things were going down the way they were and he couldn't communicate to anyone.

The night before his funeral service I was getting ready for bed. I was telling Kerry how upset I was and pissed off myself at the turn of events of the past week and a half. It was unfair and Steve should be here. He was only a year younger than me and should not be gone from us all. As I slid the dial for my alarm on my clock past the radio setting to ON, "Patience" was on the radio. This was around 9:30 at night and this particular radio station didn't play this song on rotation, if ever, anymore. It was at the point in the song where the line says "Just take it slow and it will work itself out fine, all we need is just a little patience." I was stunned. I just looked up and said, "Steve, I get it, I love and will miss you and thank you!"

There was one more time a week or so later that I heard "Patience" on the radio as I turned my truck on to head out somewhere. As the song was playing I said out loud, "Steve if this is you giving me another sign, and was you giving me a sign saying you heard me at the hospital and before your funeral, please give me one more bud, that I can't call coincidence." The next song that played following "Patience" was "Sweet Melissa" from The Allman Brothers. I listen to WGIR (Rock 101) almost EVERYDAY and haven't heard that song on the radio in well over twenty-five years. I believe it was Steve and he heard me. For that, I am thankful.

In 2018, about eight months after Steve's passing, another great friend and fellow bandmate off and on since 1997 came to me to let me know he had been diagnosed with cancer. David was a talented guy whose main instrument was drums, but also played guitar, bass guitar and sang, like myself. We had a lot in common with music and who we liked for bands and musical influences. As David was going through his treatments there came a time when he decided he wanted to get together with our other great friend, former bandmate & die-hard KISS fan like ourselves, Vinny. Dave wanted to play & sing music until he couldn't and asked me and Vinny if we would be open to jamming KISS songs on a weekly basis. We, of course, agreed as it was important time being spent with our friend. Near the last month of Dave's life, some great friends of mine had a private box at the Boston Garden and invited me to bring Dave along for the night to see the reunited Guns N' Roses concert. I am also still greatly appreciative for my friends offer and this night, as David and I had a great time together with a lot of heartfelt conversations throughout the night. I did have a moment thinking of Steve as GN'R was playing "Patience." David asked me If I wanted and would take his drum set as a token of our friendship, musical passion we shared as bandmates, and his parting gift. He said to me, "Jéan, I expect you to play my drums and keep my musical voice alive after I'm gone."

"Dave," I said, "I will do that before you're gone so you can see your drum kit on a stage again before you have to leave."

"Done deal!" he exclaimed.

I went to meet David to pick up his drums from a dilapidated storage shed. After the drums were loaded in my truck we had another heartfelt conversation but this one broke us both. It brought us to tears and hugging each other. Dave told me his time was running out as he was feeling more frail, tired, and was told by doctors there was nothing left they could do for him. I told him, "between you and I, let's pick a sign you can give me after you've passed so I know you're around, with me, or can hear me if I talk to you." He said, "We're connected musically and by drums. How about I give you a drum noise?"

"PERFECT!" I said. "See you on Tuesday to jam." He nodded and said, "RIGHT! See ya then." Tuesday came and Vinny, David and myself played through the KISS song set. It was evident that Vinny and I could see Dave's deterioration. His playing was getting worse as the months went by.

He was a perfectionist and had a bit of a temper. He would get really mad at something he couldn't play correctly or would make a mistake playing. By this point, we could barely get through any of the songs without an issue and Dave would get pissed at himself. The cancer had spread to his brain and he just couldn't remember things anymore. His determination to succeed never wavered.

Usually, after we jammed for a while, Vinny and Dave would say their goodnight and leave. This night was different. Dave stayed and had chili that Kerry had made for dinner. He stayed much longer than normal but later we realized he didn't want to go. David knew we wouldn't be jamming again because he couldn't do it and didn't want to tell us or quit. This would be the last night we saw David. The following Monday, Dave sent Vinny and I a text saying he was moving up north with his sister and brother in-law. He needed more care and couldn't be by himself anymore. He said, "we'll get together next

Tuesday." I had a show in Buffalo, New York on Friday night and was going to surprise David with his drum set on the stage. I had cleaned it up, rebuilt and ordered parts for it and had it ready to go. On my eight hour drive out to Buffalo, I called Dave a couple times with no answer. I left a message that I had a surprise for him and would text him some pictures later that night. I figured David was sleeping or busy and I'd hear back from him later that day. I arrived at the venue and had Dave's drums all set up and looking fantastic. I took a couple pictures and texted them to him and was anxiously awaiting his response. I figured he'd be happy and I'd get a "HELL YEAH BROTHER!" Nothing! Nothing ever came. Now I started to get a bit nervous. It was unlike him to not reply. I started thinking the worst. After the show was done, I headed back to the hotel parking garage to drop off my truck and get some sleep before the long drive home in the morning.

As I approached my truck the next morning my stomach dropped. Somebody had smashed out the back window of my truck bed cap to steal my gear. My drums. DAVE's DRUMS! I always park against a wall or something so that if this situation ever happened, the thieves would not be able to get my tailgate down and to limit what they'd be able to make off with. Now the odd thing is, after the show, I completely packed my truck differently than usual in a rush to leave the venue. All the big things like the bass drum were closest to the tailgate when usually it's backwards and the smaller drums and cases are closest to the tailgate. The thieves couldn't get anything out through the broken window because it was all large cases. The only thing that was missing was a suitcase that held our band merchandise. On the drive back home Saturday morning, I received a text and call from another good friend of Dave's that was also a former bandmate of mine and Vinny's. Zander had seen David the day before my show on Thursday. He told me not long after he had left, at some point between Thursday and my drive on Friday morning out to Buffalo, David had become unresponsive and he eventually passed a couple days later. He never got my messages, texts or the pictures of his drum kit (Big Red) on that stage.

The following weekend a bunch of friends that were also close to Dave got together at my house to have a "Let's celebrate and remember David" night and hang. Everyone shared stories of great times we had with Dave - there were many funny ones, and luckily enough, many are on video so that we can revisit them. I started telling everyone gathered in my kitchen of the night I went to pick up David's drums and the moment we had crying together knowing he was going to have to leave soon. I explained the sign that Dave and I picked out. No sooner than I said it, there was a "bing" sound on an upside down pan in the dish strainer. Everybody went silent. You could hear a pin drop. Our friend Jerry said, "Way to go, Dave! Can you do something else?" Immediately after Jerry asked, the pan that the metallic sound came from moved by itself slightly in the strainer. Lauri said out loud, "Thank you David and we love and miss you!" A few days later, I was in my basement studio getting ready to rehearse some new songs that the band was planning to add to our set. I sat behind the drums and just as I was reaching for my drum sticks I heard two little taps on the floor tom of the drum set. I stopped moving and still didn't have my sticks in hand. I never got to them before I heard the drum noise. "Dave, do it again," I asked. "Tap Tap!" My heart got heavy with sadness because he was gone but I was happy because he was still around.

L to R : Vinny, myself, David and Jerry.
Friends for life and in death.

The final David interaction from the other side happened to me and Vinny together. We were recording a Peter Criss/KISS Tribute album called "Faith & Will Vol. 1" in my studio. The album was done to generate proceeds to go to individuals or families of KISS fans dealing with their fight with cancer. This is something that Vinny and I found extremely personal as both my mother, his father and now David had passed from. Cancer is just evil! We added a song that David sang background vocals on that we had done about ten years before on the album. We were talking about Dave and how we wished he was around to be a part of this now instead of what we had recorded long ago. We knew David would want to be a part of this project. Not sure who said this, but either Vinny or myself said "If Dave could see this he'd probably be pissed off that he's not here to be involved in the recording." We kind of chuckled then "Tap Tap" on the floor tom of the drums again. We were ten feet away from where the drums were. We looked at each other and I said, "Vin did you hear that?" He said "Yeah, I did. It was probably a vibration or something." he exclaimed.

"Vinny, he's here. I know it!" I said. "Maybe he is pissed." Just then, the huge, heavy, wooden door to the studio slammed closed. Almost as if Dave just left the studio aggravated that he wasn't involved. That would have been the perfect action he would have done in life if he was there and we told him we didn't want to use him on a certain song that he wanted to be on. Vinny looked at me and said, "Now that was unmistakable. I saw that!"

I still wonder if David actually saw his drum kit set up in Buffalo before he passed or saved it from being stolen from me. I still feel at times he and Steve are still around, but I wish it was more. They were great friends and people that are truly missed daily by many of us.

Chapter 14

Shadow People And Paranormal On The Road

Have you ever seen a shadow movement out of the corner of your eye and thought it was a person but when you turned there was no one there? I will bet that more often than not it certainly was someone. Just not someone in the same realm and plane as you. It's been said that shadow figures or shadow people are people that have passed over but are not at rest. Some re-live their whole lives again but on a different level and at times we just happen to catch a glimpse of their movement and actions. It's also been said that these paranormal occurrences are not intellectual hauntings and just a soul of the deceased doing what they did when they were alive. It's like watching a movie on a VHS tape and when it gets to the end, it rewinds and replays. The entity doesn't know you are there and they go about their business. Now, on the other hand, some shadow people are also said to be on the malevolent side and are able to cross over to our realm and cause fear, uncomfortableness and chaos.

In my house, many times I've seen shadows move along

the walls or in rooms. These aren't shadows of the cat or dog walking by a light. These are solid mass, black shadows that block out the background as they move about. As an example, I've seen dark shadow figures that are of human shape walk by a window and block the window and the scenery outside completely for a moment. Same as a moving shadow across a wall that blocks out a picture on the wall for a split second as it moves past and in front of it. A friend stayed over at our house one night because she didn't want to drive home. It was really late, or early morning depending how you look at the time. She told me and Kerry the next morning that she had a weird occurrence. "Hey guys," she said, "A really strange thing happened last night. Did one of you come back downstairs last night to check on me?"

"No we didn't," Kerry said, "Why do you ask?"

"Well, because I was just laying there with my eyes closed and felt like someone was standing over me. The darkness with my eyes closed got darker like a face got closer to mine. I stayed still like I was asleep for a minute or so and when I opened my eyes no one was there. I didn't hear any movement or footsteps coming down the stairs or around in the room."

Then there was another time I remember when we had friends over for a fire pit hangout in the backyard. My friend went into the house to use the bathroom and came out of the house quickly with a look of confusion on his face. When we asked what was the matter, the reply was "What the Fuck!"

"What's up?" I asked. He replied, "When I was walking down the hallway towards the bathroom, I saw a really tall, black figure in the living room. As I got closer to the bathroom it disappeared. Dude," he said to me, "That was freaky and uncomfortable." This was the same room where our other friend had slept on the couch. Another friend was over at my house and we were hanging out in the kitchen just chatting. He was playing ball with the dog, rolling a tennis ball down the hallway and the dog would fetch it and bring it back. One of the times, the ball got knocked into the dining room. The dog did not go into the room to get it. The room was completely dark and no one or nothing was in the room. About five minutes after the ball went in the room, the tennis ball came rolling back into the kitchen by my friend's feet and next to the dog.

This is the same room, that many years before, I had seen my father's shadow in the window when I was in the car with Katie parked out in front of the house. Was it the same entity? Was it "Little boy" or "Alexander" playing with the dog? I don't know if all the shadow people we've seen are the same person or various people. Not sure how many spirits, entities or ghosts are in my house with us but I can say without a doubt it's not just the two of us. It has been common over the years that Kerry and I have seen shadow figures in our house. Our friends or family visiting have seen them also. Another thing to note is a lot of these particular friends didn't know each other, as these incidents happened over the course of twenty years. There was no way they knew what the others had experienced.

A few other interesting things have happened in hotels while I was traveling on tour over the past twenty years. There was a time that I was rooming with Sean (Lead vocalist in SCARAB) in a hotel in South Carolina. It was after the show we had just played. We got some food to bring back to the room, chill out a bit and unwind as we usually did after performing. We would watch old 70's sitcoms or "Seinfeld" which was a favorite if we got lucky enough and it was on. We were watching TV and above the TV on the wall was a large, framed picture. The picture just tilted to one side by itself very slowly. We looked at each other and I asked, "DID YOU SEE THAT?" The reply I got was, "How could you not!" The next morning, little things we had out on the dresser that the TV was on were moved around or missing – my wallet, spare change and his inhaler. It was the oddest thing. We didn't do any of it but somebody certainly did.

A couple years ago, Ron (The lead vocalist in WILD-SIDE) and I went out to California for a music convention. It is an annual trade show which is organized by the National Association of Music Merchants (NAMM), which describes it as "the industry's largest stage, uniting the global music, sound and entertainment technology communities." We were staying at The Kings Inn in Anaheim. Ron and I are both pranksters and always out to get comic relief from each other or some unknowing participant. From the time we flew out of Logan International Airport in Boston to landing in California, it was "Game On!" Ron caught me dozing off on the plane, which I usually never do. I was really overtired for whatever reason. He put a cup on the visor of my hat and snapped a picture that he'd text me a day later. I had no idea, but we laughed as always.

We went out for dinner and a walk about the area. I had been out there many times but it was Ron's first time at the convention. We finally rolled back to the hotel room to get some sleep after a long day of traveling and various shenanigans. I was just about to fall asleep and was in the relaxed state, yet still aware I was awake. I felt the mattress compress down on the side of my leg near the edge of the bed. My mind went into hyper-overdrive because I figured Ron just sat on the bed next to me thinking I was asleep and was going to punk me somehow. Well, little did he know I was still awake. I wasn't going to let him get me again, and I owed him after the cup on the visor on the plane. I sat up as fast as I could to grab him and get him in the chest and throw him off my bed. To my surprise, I almost threw my shoulder out of the socket because no one was there. When I opened my eyes, he was asleep and lightly snoring across the room from me on a roll- away cot. There's no way he could have gotten back there without me seeing him. His blanket was over him and he was down for the count. This whole episode took a total of maybe less than two minutes. I was dumbfounded.

I told Ron the next day and his eyes went wide. "REALLY?" he said. He was blown away and thought I was just joking with him. I was not! We decided to walk over to the convention center. I figured I'd show Ron around the area, and where the music entertainment and parties would be for the weekend. The exhibitors were still setting up in the convention halls. There were crates of music gear and pallets all over the place. Fork trucks were moving the participating companies gear for their booths to their places. This particular NAMM Show was much smaller than most, as it was the year after the pandemic. People were still not ready to gather in large crowds yet and afraid of being infected by the virus. The convention floor and halls were condensed and the whole show was expected to be only at sixty five percent compared to decades of shows before this. As we walked throughout the convention hall floor we could see how they had downsized and sectioned off areas that were not going to be used that normally would be. They ended up using the inside area behind the curtains for crate and pallet storage for companies until the breakdown after the show was over on Sunday.

Ron and I were walking in an area where there was absolutely no one and taking a short cut to stay out of the way of people setting up their booths. We carefully stayed away from the many fork lift trucks moving quickly around the floor. All of a sudden we heard a small thud type of noise and a water bottle came rolling out from behind a large concrete pillar holding the ceiling up. There was absolutely no one around and no machinery near us. We looked quickly on the other side of the pillar but there was nothing but a couple of stacked pallets. The convention floor is concrete so there was no vibration under our feet.

Where did this bottle come from? Who knocked it over and rolled it right in front of our feet? Was this the same ghost that sat on my bed the previous night? Was it someone that either one of us might know? Could it be someone just saying hi and "Hey.. We're with you?" I don't have any answers to these questions.

Another time, while out in California for the NAMM show at a different hotel I was staying at with a former member of BOTTOMS UP, a strange incident happened. I was laying in bed and was in that state where you're awake but just on the edge of falling asleep. I was laying on my side facing the wall and my bed was the one closest to the door. All of a sudden, in one swoop, all my blankets, including the sheet, were ripped off me and fell on the floor at the foot of the bed. I sat up quickly and turned over, figuring I'd catch my friend climbing back into bed after pranking me. He was sound asleep and snoring. I figured he was faking being asleep so I shook him and said "Good one! You got me!" He rolled over, woke up and was pissed at me that I awoke him from his sound slumber.

"What the hell are you talking about? You just woke me up!" He said this in a very stern and annoyed voice. I apologized for waking him, put my covers back on my bed and crawled back in.

As I laid there thinking about what just happened, something occurred to me. He couldn't have pulled the blankets off of me, raced around my bed, got back into his, turned over and pulled his blankets up to his neck without me seeing him. He wouldn't have even made it to his bed yet. I mean, I turned over immediately once my blankets slid off me. It was so quick, like the tablecloth trick that leaves all the table settings on the table after it's pulled out from underneath at lightning speed. I guess it's a good thing I don't sleep naked. That would have been embarrassing.

Chapter 15

A Bright Light Shines In The Night

On May 7th, 2024, Kerry awoke in the early morning hours from her sleep. As she was walking down the second floor hallway from the bedroom to the bathroom, she noticed a light illuminating from the bottom of the stairs. That light was coming from a battery-operated candle that was inside the top of a large lighthouse. My mother loved lighthouses and this large red and white striped lighthouse was used as the table centerpiece for the party we had for my mom on that Valentine's day that I mentioned previously. After the party and after my mom had passed, Kerry had made a beautiful memorial garden in our yard. It consisted of different items that represented our family and friends that have passed on, some that were mentioned in the previous chapters.

This large lighthouse was placed outside from spring until fall. We brought it in the house during the winter and colder months so it wouldn't endure any type of damage. Kerry had placed a battery- operated candle in the top that was on a twelve hour timer. It was set to turn on at

6pm and turn off at 6am. My mother passed away on May 9th, 2016 around 6pm. When I would let the dog out at night to do his business before going to bed, I'd see the lighthouse lit up, smile, and think some thought about me and my mom. Eventually, near the end of the fall season in 2018, the batteries died in the candle light. The lighthouse went dark in the night. We brought the lighthouse in the house and it sat at the bottom of our stairs near the front door. We never took the batteries out of the candle. We meant to, but just got busy and forgot about it. Thankfully the batteries didn't start to leak acid. For five or so years the lighthouse was dark, until that night that Kerry was shocked to see it lit up.

She came back into the bedroom to wake me up. "Jéan!" she said, "You have to get out of bed and come and see this. I think your mom has come back to visit us. The lighthouse downstairs is lit up." I reluctantly got out of bed as I like my sleep. I'm a bit of an insomniac so when I am actually getting restful sleep, I'm not a fan of being woken up. I got out of bed and saw the candle on. I was still half-asleep so I didn't get the full picture at that moment. "Yeah, the light is on. It comes on at six and goes off at six, right? So it would be on now." At that moment, I wasn't as excited as she was to see the light beaming from the bottom of the stairs. "Kerry, I need sleep. We can chat about this in a few hours."

When I awoke and came into the kitchen in the morning, Kerry was standing there waiting for me. "How cool was that last night? Wasn't that unbelievable that the candle was on?" She said excitedly. "It's off now as it would be because it's past 6am," I stated.

"Jéan!" she said, "The batteries in that candle are dead. That light hasn't come on for almost five years! Have you ever noticed it on lately, or at all?"

"No, as a matter of fact, I haven't. I honestly don't really notice or pay that close attention, but I can say I haven't noticed it on." As I went off to work I kept thinking, maybe there could be something to this. That's when I realized the date was only two days prior to the date of my mother's death. Was she coming back to to let us know she was still around on occasion? I needed to know.

When I arrived back home from work that afternoon, I had a thought. I needed to see if I could talk to my mother and if she would answer by turning the candle light on, but on command.

As I sat in my office chair at my computer desk, I glanced over at the lighthouse. The lighthouse was only three feet away from me. I asked out loud, "Mom, if you turned the candle on in the lighthouse last night, can you turn it on again for me right now?" Not more than five seconds after I asked the question the light turned on. I was floored to say the least. I quickly grabbed my cell phone and put it on video. I asked again, "Mom, can you turn the light off now?" Another five to seven seconds went by and the light went off. I can't even convey the different emotions that just washed over me at that moment. The thoughts in my head were bouncing everywhere. I tried this call and answer to my mother again, asking her to turn the light on and off again. She achieved it again. I said out loud, "OH MY GOD! Thank you mom and I love and miss you." As I sat in my chair dumbfounded by what just transpired I realized, this was an even more amazing sequence of events. When I conducted this session with my mom (at the time, I was hopeful it was in fact my mother communicating with me) it hit me like a ton of bricks... That candle is set for the twelve hour on/off cycle for 6pm to 6am. That candle should technically have not been able to illuminate! It wasn't during the "on" time and the batteries were dead. Was my mother's energy enough to give the batteries enough power to turn on the candle? I was so shocked, yet excited, I needed to text Kerry and let her know what had just happened.

When Kerry arrived home from work, I explained in detail to her everything that happened. What I did, what I said, and the outcome of the light coming on and going off as I requested. "It's got to be her," I said. Kerry grabbed her cell phone and started to video record. She pointed the phone at the lighthouse. The candle was not lit. "What are you doing?" I asked. She said to me, "Tell me the story again and let's see if something happens."

"Ok," I replied. I repeated the story to Kerry, "So I asked

my mom to turn on the light." Just as I said that, the
lighthouse candle turned on.

My mother's lighthouse

Kerry was blown away, as was I, yet again. She exclaimed out loud, "Carol, it's pretty freakin' cool that you can do that. Can you turn the light off now?" The light turned off immediately after Kerry's request was made. We tried to do this again, but nothing. I guess my mom was tired. As we watched TV, I kept looking at the lighthouse during the commercial breaks. The light didn't come back on.

We went to bed, but the cats woke Kerry up in the early morning, a little before her alarm was to go off. The cats get pushy in the morning when they want breakfast, and will do whatever they need to wake us. Kerry got up and when she got to the top of the stairs she looked down to see the lighthouse was glowing. She came back into the bedroom to let me know the candle was lit. I got up, saw it, and climbed back into bed for another hour. When I finally came downstairs on the morning of May 9th, the light was off. So strange. We went about our normal morning routines and both headed off to work. When I arrived home in the afternoon after work, I sat in my office chair and peered over to the lighthouse. "Mom, if this is really you lighting up the candle, please light it up again right now." Sure enough, in less than ten seconds the light came on. Again, it was the middle of the afternoon and the timer is not set for the light to be able to turn on. I'm very thankful all of this was caught on video. It was simply amazing.

Later that evening, Kerry I were watching TV. Around 7:30pm, that candle turned on and my mom's lighthouse was lit up. It stayed on all night and was on when we went upstairs to go to sleep. I woke up around 5am and the candle was still on as I could see from the top of the stairs. I said out loud, "Mom, if that is you doing this, thank you for visiting us on the anniversary of you leaving us. It makes me feel comfort knowing you're still around us when you can be. Now since that candle is set to turn off at 6am, if you can shut it off by 5:30, before I come back down the stairs, I will know and believe all these signs over the past few days were definitely from you." I proceeded to get dressed and get ready to head downstairs. As I got to the landing and looked down at the lighthouse, the light was off. She turned it off between 5:12am and 5:22am, well before the 6am timed shut off.

We did our morning routines and headed off to work. When I arrived home, I again asked her to turn the light on. It didn't turn on and it hasn't come back on since those episodes. What I find intriguing, is that spirits can drain power sources, like batteries. They can also add energy to drained batteries, just allowing enough energy to power them for a short time. I really want to believe we had communication from my mother and hope to again. Maybe it will happen next May. If it wasn't my mother and was some other entity messing with us it still proves two things: one) spirits of the deceased still try to communicate with the living, two) if it wasn't my mother, you fooled me, but you also made me feel comfort in believing my mom is doing well wherever she may be. For that, I am thankful.

I don't have any answers to any of the paranormal incidents I've witnessed over my lifetime so far. I probably do have many more encounters that I could write in another book. As I'm finishing this one, I turned fifty-seven. The Ouija board that forewarned back in the late eighties that I would pass at either fifty-four or fifty-six was wrong. Well, it was almost right as I did have a health issue that caused me to collapse and turn blue at fifty-six. I've had more than a few situations in my life when I've come close to death but always seem to make it through. My nine lives have to be getting close to the end, but whoever is watching over me has given me a few passes to continue on with my life. My guardian angel has been working overtime for many years. I have to say, I appreciate it though I would like to have my paranormal questions answered. If I have to die to know the true meaning of life or just *my* life, I can wait a bit longer. I have so much more I'd like to do, and I'm sure more paranormal oddities to witness.

I sometimes wish I understood the strange gift I have so I could communicate with my family and friends that have passed on more often, and how to use it more to my ability. However, like I mentioned earlier, unless I can get winning lottery numbers, I'm not sure I want to delve into it more. It's a bit unnerving at times but I'll accept what I have and what happens. Hopefully when my time, your time and everyone's time comes to move on to the next chapter of our existence, we will be guided by our family and friends that already know the answers and can show us the way. I encourage everyone that's missing someone special in their life that has passed to be open to receiving signs meant for you. Talk to them. Ask them for help or signs that could help you with your life and decisions. Will you get the answers? Nothing is guaranteed, except death and taxes. Is it worth a shot to take a chance? I believe it is. I was a skeptic until there was proof before me eyes, ears, mind and validation from my aunt (The Catholic Nun), that there is more going on around us everyday. While I certainly don't claim to be an expert in the paranormal field, I felt the need to share my stories about the paranormal happenings that I've witnessed. Maybe it's happening to you, or someone that you know, or maybe this book will help or validate your own experiences. I don't have the answers to how and why, but then again nobody truly does. It's all speculation as to what's after this world we live in. Is the paranormal, ghosts, spirits, poltergeists, shadow people and afterlife real? I believe one hundred and ten percent that they all exist.

They could be trying to communicate with you also.

Acknowledgements

Thank You

Kerry Grenier, Tammy Messier, Vinny Nault,
Jerry Hannon, Laurianne Brown, Bob Brown,
Ron Finn, Scott Draper, Mary Wood,
Larry Kanan, Debi King
Hope Cheney Parker, Brett Parker,
Sean Volpetti, Nina Walden,
Lisa Dowaliby, Erica Brickley,
BOTTOMS UP Band
SCARAB (The Journey Experience) Band
WILDSIDE (80's Hard Rock Tribute) Band
You've all given me support, encouragement and/or have
been a part of my paranormal journey in some aspect.
Without your help, assistance and time, this book likely
would never have gotten finished.
Thank you so very much and I appreciate you all!

Photo Credits

Foreword Photo (Jéan & Lisa Dowaliby) : Kerry Grenier

(Grenier Family) : Authors Archives

(Sister Antoinette Grenier) : Authors Archives

(Jéan in Smokey & The Bandit Trans Am) :
Photographer Unknown

(Abel Blood Sr. Tombstone) :
Google Search (Uploaded By – Venusblue)

(Sarah Blood Tombstone) : Jéan Boomer Grenier

(Jéan 1987) : Photographer Unknown

(Jéan & Kerry 1994) : Edith Fusco

(Cracked Front Door) : Jéan Boomer Grenier

(Jéan & Mary Ouija Board) : Kerry Grenier

(Jéan & Father) : Carol Grenier

(Jéan & Chris) : Authors Archives

(Jéan, Kerry & Mom) : Hope Cheney Parker

(Jéan & Michele) : Kerry Grenier

(Footprints) : Jéan Boomer Grenier

(Jéan & Steve) : Mary King

(Vinny, Jéan, David & Jerry) : Kerry Grenier

(Lighthouse) : Jéan Boomer Grenier
(Jéan Live Shot) : Hope Cheney Parker
Back Cover Photo Of Jéan : Michael Hacala

About The Author

Jéan Boomer Grenier has been a musician since the age of nine years old. Music became a passion and drums became his musical voice. Later learning to play guitar and bass guitar, Jéan began writing and recording his own songs and music. He has been a touring musician with many bands over the past forty-one years, playing on stages both nationally and internationally. He has performed on many worldwide album releases and continues to release new music and perform to this day.
He is still currently with the bands, BOTTOMS UP & WILDSIDE (The Hard Rock 80's Tribute).

Jéan enjoys spending time with his family, his fur kids and friends. When not performing, he enjoys riding his motorcycle, kayaking, camping and traveling with his wife. These are among his favorite hobbies and pastimes.

Writing this book also became a passion. There seems to be a need for validation, closure and acceptance for personal loss and of the unexplained that can manifest in all our lives. While some of these experiences for Jéan were shocking, scary and unsettling, there is also validation and closure of what he knows to be true through his eyes. Hopefully this book may help validate an experience for you and give you hope, peace and closure, if needed.

More more info & details, Please visit ;
jeanboomergrenier.com & jboomergrenier.com